Microscopes and Magic

Andi R. Christopher

Copyright page

A catalogue record for this book is available from the National Library of New Zealand.

ISBN

978-0-473-69693-1 (paperback)

978-0-473-69694-8 / 978-0-473-69695-5 (ebook)

Contents

Microscopes and Magic

Marigold Nightfield had left the paths of Otari-Wilton's Bush behind, scrambling among the ferns. It was February, a late summer's day, and the wind was - by Wellington standards at least - gentle. Marigold had been there since eight. She was normally a morning person, so it didn't feel too bad, and she had happily walked past bleary-eyed commuters and traffic queues, around the hills from the house she shared with her father. She'd carried her morning coffee in a reusable cup, and her equipment in a small backpack, thinking it would only take an hour or two but now it was midday, her mission still unsuccessful, and she'd had to slather herself in sunscreen just to keep going.

She looked around at the tangle of native bush she stood in the middle of. Otari-Wilton's was one of her favourite places–more than a thousand native species, recreated ecosystems of different parts of the country. There was a sense of the land as it once was - and as it could be - here among Wellington's hills. It was a fantastic research resource as well, though her official project focused on organisms smaller than plants.

Even with the careful attention afforded them, several of the plants she came across were wilted in the summer heat. That didn't surprise her–but the number that were outright dead did. Things just didn't seem healthy, and while she was in search of a snail rather than a plant, it didn't seem like a happy environment for them either.

The reserve was busy for a weekday - she supposed anyone who could was trying to get some time outside before the weather disintegrated - and she was getting some awkward looks. If she'd thought this through, she'd have dressed in a way that made her look like she could be maintaining the bush professionally, one of the council workers. Instead, here she was in bright floral-patterned shorts and a green t-shirt with a picture of a brachiosaur looking carefully down a microscope. She'd buzzed her hair back last week, and on top of that she had a wide-brimmed purple sun hat. She was too much of a scientist not to take sun safety seriously. Even if the hat did keep getting hooked on dry fern fronds as she made her way through the bush, forcing her to stop, fight with the ferns some more, and retrieve it. Which was not helping her search.

Fortunately, Marigold had some other methods available to her. Her magic was relatively new, but she'd been practising. She breathed in, found her power inside her then reached out her arms. The fronds of the ferns curled up before her as if it was night, opening a passage through. Marigold grinned, her first real smile after a morning of frustration. She checked the ground ahead before walking through. It wouldn't do to crush the very creature she was looking for, especially now she was finally making progress. The bush seemed to work with her, rather than against her, and she felt warm. Having magic was wonderful. She had always been fine with not being a witch–until she found out what she was missing out on.

And now that she was a witch - but not forever, perhaps not even for long - she wanted to make the most of every minute of it. She'd been working on it, pushing herself on spells that required focus until she could light a flame with her hands, move objects across her room, suspend water in mid-air.

She had not been born a witch. She had become one only because her girlfriend had given her the powers of another, powers that had been locked away for decades. She knew that even as she strengthened her abilities, the power behind them was seeping away. Not knowing how long that would take unsettled her. She liked to be able to plan, to predict, to imagine how she was going to handle things before she had to. Having so many things open-ended, so many possibilities, was at once both wonderful and stressful. She knew she was lucky, but she was finding anxiety she thought she had got under control years ago seeping through.

Which was probably why she was in Otari-Wilton's Bush on a summer Tuesday lunchtime, searching for a magical snail. Research was how Marigold dealt with stress. She thought quickly. Snails emerge when it's wet, she knew that much. The spell that came to mind was at the edge of her abilities, but she felt she could pull it off. She said the incantation under her breath...

...and was immediately hit by a high-pressure jet of water, right in the face, as if someone had turned a hose directly on her. She swore, desperately searching her memory for some kind of reversal spell, turning and trying to duck away through the ferns. No matter what she did the water seemed to be aimed directly at her.

"Hi!"

The water stopped, immediately. Marigold blinked a couple of times to get it from her eyes. When she opened them, she saw a hand clutched into a fist, as if it had just shut off the jet of water. She focused and saw Laurel, her girlfriend of six months, standing among the ferns. Her blue hair was bobbed short for summer and she was wearing a matching blue summer dress with small white flowers, and jandals on her feet. Six months of seeing each other most days and Marigold still felt a rush of happiness when she appeared.

"Uh, hi Laurel, I'm just..."

"My fault. I should never have taught you any spells without how to put an end to them. You okay?"

Marigold brushed herself off and squeezed water from her t-shirt. Her clothes were drenched.

"I am now. Thanks."

"I brought a picnic. Let's head over to one of the tables and take a break."

Marigold dried off easily in the summer sun, and there was still one picnic table free, onto which Laurel unloaded cheese sandwiches, homemade sushi, and cold American lemonade from a swap she'd made for herbs.

"You're amazing!" Marigold said, shaking off her t-shirt to help it dry faster.

"It's a celebration," Laurel said. "I handed in my notice today."

Marigold yelled in excitement and they hi-fived with both hands, causing a few looks from the other picnickers.

"Two weeks?"

"Yeah, and then I am out of that place! Then the student loan kicks in and it's that and what I make from my business. Money may be a bit tight for a while, but it's a weight lifted off my shoulders, it really is."

"And it will be good to finish your thesis."

"Yeah. I know it's not the direction I want to go in anymore, but having the thing hanging over me was just bringing me down. I need to finish what I've started. I reckon if I put my head down I can get it done around the end of first semester. And it will be nice being on campus, we can get coffee."

Marigold nodded, chewing on a sandwich. She had more mixed feelings about the academic year starting, the hordes of students pushing their way through the corridors or - worse - standing obliviously in the middle of them. She was excited about tutoring first-year labs again, that brief time when they had not yet gained the veneer of cynicism that most students eventually succumb to, and were excited to be there, having escaped from god knows what small towns.

Her own research though, wasn't going to plan. The results of her studies - examining ways bacteria became anti-biotic resistant and the resultant changes in their structure - were all over the place. No matter how many people told her it was normal to be behind at this point, and she would be just fine, she was struggling to believe it.

She did her best to put those worries aside for now though. Taking a lunch break wouldn't make things any worse, the weather was glorious and her girlfriend - and she felt her heart skip a beat at that word - was sitting opposite her, pouring out lemonade into plastic tumblers.

"So, snails proving elusive?"

"Every time I've been here I've seen one!" Marigold bemoaned. "Every single time except the one time I want to analyse one. Maybe they're deliberately avoiding me. Maybe they don't want any of their slime put on a microscope slide."

"It is possible," Laurel admitted. "So what exactly does this snail slime do? And don't you have enough research projects?"

Marigold laughed. "Have you *met* me? No such thing as too many research projects. But in this specific case, it's not my research. I'm helping out a contact in Chile. She's very cool, doing all this research into magical invertebrates - or more specifically those who have magical secretions. She's been able to find a surprising number locally, but this one is apparently special and she wants to include it in her research."

"I like how you're building this magical science network."

Marigold opened a plastic container and helped herself to raspberry and coconut slice. She was usually the baker, but Laurel seemed to be doing more of it these days.

"Yeah, it's really nice to be part of it. We can support each other's work in different ways, advice about how to get real outcomes while still being a bit under the radar, and, well, we sometimes get to go on weird snail catching expeditions for each other."

"We'll have a look after lunch," Laurel said. "Hopefully together we can find it. Do you have a picture?"

The picture Marigold showed Laurel on her phone was blurry and out of focus; it was hard to even tell it was a snail, but Marigold at least pointed out a few characteristics, particularly the bright red speckling of its shell, and the areas it had been sighted in before.

"Don't suppose you have any good spells to help us out?" Marigold said, hope not evident in her voice.

Laurel shook her head.

"Not with the things I have on me, at least, but I can sometimes sense magic. Might draw me closer to it, worth a try. In any case, two eyes are better than..."

"Four," Marigold said resolutely. "Four eyes are better than two."

"Marigold," Laurel said. "I will never stop loving your courageous insistence on accuracy." She raised her tumbler of homemade lemonade.

"To the truth!" Marigold said, dramatically, and they both laughed, but she felt something else inside, something she couldn't quite define. She wasn't used to people *liking* her weirdness; the best she had ever been able to hope for was being liked in spite of it.

They found the snail more easily than Marigold had expected after that, and without any apparent use of magic. Perhaps it was indeed that four eyes were better than two, or perhaps she was buoyed by Laurel's company, her enthusiasm and energy restored. Either way, she saw it when she almost wasn't trying, the brown shell speckled with red and about the size of a bottle cap. She took out one of her pre-prepared containers and, apologising as she did so, gently plucked it from the branch and placed it inside. She had a small habitat already ready at home, and she would keep it there until her contact had received the slides and confirmed they had what they needed.

She didn't suppose the snail would mind too much, once it got over the initial shock.

Laurel and Marigold returned to the pathway and brushed the various bits of soil and plant matter from their clothes.

"Connor and I are making enchiladas for dinner," Laurel said. "You're welcome to join us."

"Thanks but I said I'd cook for Dad. We're still good for that play tomorrow though?"

"Yeah... this is going to be one of your weird ones, isn't it?"

Marigold grinned and said nothing.

"Fine," said Laurel, whose tastes were always more traditional in everything except perhaps hair colour. "I'll make you sit through King Lear or something in revenge."

"I *like* Lear," Marigold insisted. "I saw a version in Berlin where all the characters were rabbits and the three daughters were the only survivors after the introduction of myxomatosis, yknow, playing with the whole thing where it was written during the plague, and there was a sentient clock and..."

Laurel shook her head in despair, jumped forward to kiss Marigold on the lips, and they headed for the entrance. Marigold waited at the bus stop with Laurel until the bus arrived, and then began walking up over the hills to home which wasn't far away, but Wellington geography made a bit of a walk. When she reached her house, she walked through her well laid out herb garden to get to the front door.

"Home!" she yelled, as she opened the door and pulled her boots off. It had taken some getting used to, the past few weeks, after a year of living in an empty house and having her apartment before that.

"Any luck?" her father called out from his study.

"Snail success!" she said, pushing open the door and showing the container. The room was, in contrast to the rest of the house, chaos–drawings pinned up on the walls, books overflowing the bookcase and piled up on the floor.

"Yes, very good, please make sure it doesn't escape. You're quite enough pest for one house."

"Charming. Remember I'm cooking tonight and have the ability to poison you."

"You've been talking about poisoning me since you were eighteen months old... you'd have already done it by now if you were planning to."

"Yeah, fine, okay. How was your day?"

"Uninspiring. Been reviewing some plans for a colleague. I need to get started on the book, but you know how things are... coffee?"

"Yup. And take those cups through," Marigold said, pointing at the cluster that seemed to be reproducing on the desk.

"Jeez. I go away for a year and come back to find you're the parent."

He picked up the cups, made Marigold and himself coffee, and they sat on the sofa talking. Marigold hadn't decided, yet, whether she would keep living here—she was contributing to bills (even though her father said she didn't have to) but not paying rent, and she couldn't afford anything nice on her scholarship money but... when she was seventeen she had been desperate to get out, found it stifling. House-sitting for her father had worked great, but now he was back she worried about what patterns she'd fall into, found herself pre-emptively defensive sometimes or asking permission for things she didn't need to. She wasn't sure it was good for her, but she'd probably be heading overseas for postdoc, so it seemed she may as well stay here until she finished her PhD.

If she ever finished her PhD.

Marigold sighed. Maybe she should go into the research institute and do some work tonight. Everyone expected postgrads to be pulling late nights, but so far she'd only done it because she got interested in something and didn't notice the time until it was morning, not because she'd forced herself to. But things were getting near crunch time now, so she supposed she would have to get her act together.

Easier said than done, but she'd got this far.

In her downstairs lab, she gently encouraged the snail to slither over some blank slides, and prepared them for her contact. Said contact had done the research on biosecurity rules, which were, fortunately, less strict than they were in New Zealand, and Marigold wrote the details on the package as instructed, booked the courier pick up, and left the package by the door as instructed. Then she started making pizza dough in the breadmaker, putting her laptop on the kitchen bench so she could read through some more articles for the side issue that had recently come up in her research. She stayed there leaning against the bench, refilling her coffee as needed, until it was time to make dinner, roasting pumpkin and kumara and red onion to put on the pizza. Carb central, and she made no apologies for it.

At least she'd managed to achieve *something* that day.

The play was, as Laurel had anticipated, one of Marigold's 'weird ones'. What could she say–it was part of the Fringe so not unexpected, and maybe Marigold just wasn't into realism. It didn't interest her, didn't make her brain work. The point of art was to move *away* from the real. If you were going to focus on reality why on earth wouldn't you be doing science instead?

This particular one was set in a park and had the cast as pigeons demanding bread from the audience. Even Laurel laughed, though she shook her head at the same time, not understanding what was going on *at all*. It didn't matter. They didn't have to have everything in common as a couple, and the important thing was they were willing to give each other's things a try, even if they weren't for them.

Marigold had never expected to be in a situation where the one thing going right in her life was her relationship, but this was a weird year.

Afterwards, they ate yakitori at a little upstairs bar; it was louder than Marigold liked but she could handle it for now and the food was definitely good.

"I think I'm going to take you to a *ballet*," Laurel said, a note of vengeance in her voice.

"Mmm, good, never been to one of those. But pretty girls spinning round in fancy skirts, I'm up for that. You'll have to explain it, of course."

"Deal," said Laurel. "I'll see what's scheduled."

They walked down to the waterfront, determined to enjoy the last of summer. A wind had picked up on the harbour, a light wind by Wellington standards, and the lights around the harbour were turned on, some reflected in the water. Marigold reached for Laurel's hand and found it, a little cold, in need of warming. Neither of them wanted these warm nights to end; it felt like they were in a place that could not last, scared of the happiness they had found fragmenting and burning out.

Marigold felt Laurel nudge her, and followed the direction of her finger. There was a child being almost dragged along, slow and reluctant but perhaps making it a game, and they were giggling and extending light from their fingers.

"You recognise them?" Marigold asked, looking down at the family, the presumed-mother with pink streaks in her hair.

Laurel shook her head.

"So," Marigold said, watching until the child and their parents disappeared. "Either there's yet another witching family in town, or someone's going to have a big shock as the child gets a bit older."

"The latter would be cool. Ideopathic witches are rare but they can usually do really unusual stuff. Provided their family are understanding, of course–fingers crossed. Hey, talking of magical children, when's Sorrel coming to stay?"

"Don't have definite plans yet, but I'm guessing over the Easter break. And they'd kill you if they heard you refer to them as a child."

Sorrel was Laurel's cousin–first cousin once removed, technically, but Laurel's family ignored things like that. Marigold had met them when they had visited for Christmas, and invited them to stay during a school holiday, to Laurel's slight annoyance that staying with *her* was not authorised.

Marigold had picked up on that annoyance but had no idea what to do with it. She understood Laurel's point of view, but they were going to spend the time together anyway, and Marigold was happy to be integrated into Laurel's large haphazard family; she had only her parents and a couple of cousins that she didn't really know, none of the energy and chaotic gatherings of Laurel's family. It was probably for the best - she wouldn't have coped with all of the noise when she was younger - but she still felt she was starting to get something she needed, something she had previously missed out on.

"We're going to have fun," said Laurel, and Marigold hoped her smile was genuine.

The first week of the academic year was every bit as chaotic as usual, probably more so. It hit Marigold hard; her energy felt sapped and she felt like her patience was at an edge, but she had too much to do - and more than a few meetings - for her to stay at home.

She took a deep breath. She could do this–she knew how to do this. She took the less used routes through the campus, kept her headphones on, did her best to manage her overwhelm, telling herself that things would calm down in a few weeks.

"Morning Marigold," Neha would say when she arrived. It was Neha's first day back after visiting family. She was the other PhD candidate to have started at the institute the same year as Marigold. They'd never become friends, but there was a comfort in their shared rhythms. "How are your bacteria?"

"They're still single-celled organisms with a simple internal structure. How are your Protozoa?"

"Still single-celled Eukaryotes that feed on organic matter."

The exchange hadn't been funny the first five, ten, or fifty times, but at some point after that, it had tipped over into absurdity, and they had both laughed. They laughed today too, setting themselves up, getting to work, not even mentioning their looming deadlines.

Despite being on the same campus, Marigold didn't really see Laurel until the end of the week. It didn't surprise her; she remembered those days of running round getting forms signed off, being allocated a tiny corner of shared office space, waiting for the occupational nurse to set up her chair, meeting her cohort...

Having everyone back on campus was difficult for Marigold in some ways, but she still gained a bit of enthusiasm from it–which unfortunately manifested in her lying awake thinking about her bacteria. The next morning was not as full of optimism and energy as she would have hoped, but she was determined.

She figured she'd still force herself to walk round the hills in the hope it would wake her up. She was twenty-five and not going to ask her father for a lift, nor was she going to waste money on an Uber, and the buses weren't direct. Marigold chugged coffee from her teal and orange cup as she walked, considering the central conundrum of her life: she had *too many projects*.

It was not a *new* conundrum, but it seemed to have got worse. She'd always had competing interests, but now the two main aspects of her life had tight timeframes. Her PhD, on the one hand - where postponements were possible but came with implications - and her magic, which had no extensions, and not even a predictable end date.

She needed to do her PhD–it was her career plan, everything she'd worked for, and it had the potential to set her up long after her magic was just a distant memory. But how could she have been given a gift as significant as magic, and not make the absolute most of it while she had the chance? Then there was Laurel in her life–this relationship was good, it was very good, it was important, it needed nurturing. She didn't want to break it off and she didn't want to leave it to whither; she had never had anything like it before and she was now at the stage of having met Laurel's family and being trusted to host her pre-teen cousin. And she would be miserable without Laurel.

She took out a phone and made a note in her todo list: arrange catch up with Memory. Memory was her best friend from high school, the person she'd still kept as close to as each of them moved cities. Memory was a good listener, she had her head thoroughly screwed on, but... Marigold didn't quite know what she thought about magic. Whether she'd understand how much bigger a part of Marigold's life it had become.

In any case, Marigold liked her company and they were overdue a catch-up. She put her empty cup in the mesh side pocket of her backpack and sped up her pace, hoping to work off some of her frustration. This was the long route round - it was actually quicker to go down into town and then up the hill along the Terrace or through the botanic garden - but this way avoided the crowds, and allowed Marigold to feel the wind and catch the views as she walked round the city.

In some ways, she'd never wanted to leave and didn't much like the prospect that she would likely have to again, if even temporarily. She loved these hills. Besides, she prided

herself on her stamina–she wasn't ever going to be a sprint-
er, wasn't fast, but she was used to walking, completing
distances regularly that other people would balk at.

By the time she arrived at campus, she had indeed burned
off some of the frustration and was riding a temporary high
of endorphins. Even though she knew she would crash at
some point in the afternoon, it would get her through this
tutorial, lunch, and the early afternoon meeting, if nothing
else. And, she swore, she would actually get an early night
tonight, with a potion if it became necessary to calm her
thoughts. And then it was back to a sensible routine. She
could do this.

Marigold could do it and she did do it. She got through the
first week and into the second. She found her rhythm again,
mostly. A night spent at Laurel's, preceded by Malaysian
food, and a good catch-up with Memory had helped.

She started sleeping better and she got settled with the
tutorials she was teaching, booked in some slots to use the
more sought-after equipment. She got to know the new
thesis students in her department and what they were re-

searching, offered herself as a sounding board if they needed her. She fell behind with cleaning and she accepted her father's offer to cook most nights, and she took leftovers for lunch, but she knew she'd get back on track with that soon. Mostly, things started to come together.

Mostly.

Her research wasn't quite in that category. It wasn't that she wasn't making progress–she had spent a fair bit of time analysing bacterial samples, including ones with minor antibiotic resistance, which were some of the most useful for her experiments. She was writing up notes and taking advice from her supervisors, structuring everything into what was beginning to resemble an actual thesis.

She just didn't seem to be going anywhere.

She should have been on the homeward stretch by now, setting up her last experiments, starting to collate research and do write-ups, handing in full thesis chapters for feedback. She should have been looking at job opportunities, preparing to apply for postdocs, following her nose about where the funding was going and thinking about opportunities and... she wasn't.

People told her that everyone had the same issues but... that didn't help. They urged patience but all she could see was a series of deadlines coming ever closer, and she was terrified. She didn't think they could ever understand why.

She wasn't going to stop trying though. Fridays were going to be her day at home, trying to start writing up chapters. Her first one - the Friday of the second week of the academic year - she'd set up her laptop in her lab, put away everything except the heavy equipment into stackable plastic boxes so she had minimum distractions, made herself a coffee, opened a new document and tried to get to work.

She was still glaring at a blank page half an hour later when Laurel rang. That was unusual. Neither of them used the phone much - or really knew anyone who did - and Laurel knew that Marigold in particular hated phone calls. And Laurel wasn't careless with information like that; Marigold knew that if she was calling her then there must be a really good reason for it.

"What's up," Marigold asked, concerned.

"There's something wrong with my succulents. I've been pretending I can fix them but it's getting worse and I don't know what to do."

"Ok. Plants can be unpredictable sometimes. I can help you work it out."

"This was my one thing," Laurel said, her voice almost a whisper. "The one thing that actually worked for me. And now it's also my income and my future and it's all gone to pieces."

"Hey don't get ahead of yourself. It's a hiccup. You've got gardening advice, right? How about magical advice?"

"Both. Googled everything. Called up the magical garden centre in Whanganui, they referred me to experts. No-one's seen anything quite like this before."

"Bring some plants up here. I have microscopes."

"Okay... it's worth a try, I guess."

"And I'll make us lunch."

"Now that's more like it," Laurel said, and Marigold could almost hear her trying to force a note of optimism into her voice.

Marigold went through the fridge. There were still fresh bagels and there was salmon and cream cheese. From the garden, she cut some chives and some dill, chopping them ready. Making food was the way of showing she cared that she knew best. There was enough time, she felt, to bake some aniseed cookies – it was a recipe someone had shared on the off-topic channel of her magical scientist chat, and they were quick to make with her mixer.

She poked her head round the door of her father's office.

"Laurel's coming for lunch. You want me to make you something?"

"Please. It will be a working lunch for me though. Too many things to get through."

"I know the feeling."

Marigold mixed up the dough; she had just got the cookies in the oven when Laurel arrived at the door. Marigold assembled the bagels, delivering a plate to her father, and she and Laurel sat on the sofa–or in Marigold's case on the floor in front of the sofa, eating bagels while the cookies cooled. Marigold split some between them and tupperwared the rest.

"Never complaining about the food here," Laurel said.

"Haven't been doing as much baking lately, but I'm trying to get back into it. It's even easier now Dad's back. Half as much cooking, and less worrying about things going off when I'm only cooking for me most of the time." Marigold licked the last of the sugar from her fingers and jumped up. "Right. Shall we take a look at your plants then?"

The succulents did look in a state–nothing like Marigold had seen from Laurel before. They were brown at the edges, thin-leaved, almost drooping. Certainly not something she could sell. Laurel laid them out on the bench miserably in small pots–not the ones she had been getting specially made by a magical potter, but old ones. The ones she'd used before she realised what kind of a witch she was, or that she could do this in a way that she could actually turn in to a career or at least a business. They were a mishmash of old china, one a repurposed teapot. Marigold had liked the uneven look of them, but it only really worked when the succulents were healthy; it made the mismatches seem like a conscious, cosy, old fashioned choice, the mark of individuality. But now the succulents were tired and wilted, the plants and the pots just reinforced each other's short-comings.

Laurel walked over and half-fell on the beanbag beside the door, as if it were not so much the walk up from the bus stop - not far, but steep - so much as the having to think about the plants at all that had exhausted her.

"I don't think there's anything you can do. I'm sorry to waste your time."

Marigold looked at the plants. "I'm going to start by preparing some slides. I'm going to cut some thin slices first from the healthier leaves like this one here and then..." She caught up, processing Laurel's despair in her earlier comment. She stopped, her scalpel in her hand. She put everything down on the bench, pulled her gloves off, and walked over to Laurel. Laurel shifted over as Marigold sat down next to her and they sat there for a bit, squished on the corner between the door and the wall of the lab that had once been Marigold's playroom, then her study room when she was at high school, and was now configured as a private lab.

They were silent for a bit, then Laurel breathed in as if summoning some inner strength. "Okay, let's see if we can see anything through the microscope."

Marigold scrambled to her feet and resumed her work, while Laurel googled images of what one would expect thin slices of succulent to look like under a microscope. There seemed to be many possibilities depending on species and suchlike, but she supposed even having some idea in her head might help her to recognise what was wrong, especially when they compared the healthy leaves with the ones that were less so.

The leaves Marigold was slicing were just starting to have a brown tinge to the edge but were still thick with moisture. It was satisfying to see the scalpel crunch through them. The others, by contrast, were shrivelled and sometimes needed a back-and-forth motion to get the thin slices needed. But they were finished at last and Marigold put together the slides so they could take a look. Marigold puzzled over them, turning the dial to focus, looking first at one and then the other, then handing the microscope over to Laurel.

"I don't know what I'm supposed to be seeing," Laurel said, bending to peer down through the lenses.

"No. Nor am I really. We can take some photos and consult some experts but all I can see is, well, they just look really dehydrated."

Laurel shook her head. "If it was just I wasn't watering them enough it would have come up well before now. Besides, they're built to survive on so little, they wouldn't all start having trouble pretty much at once when they've evolved to manage this state over months or more."

"Right. Is it possible there's something that's preventing them from absorbing water, though, even if they are being provided with it?"

Laurel shrugged. "I guess anything's possible. But I can't see any obvious way that's likely to be the case. Maybe we should look at the roots?"

Nothing about the roots looked damaged, though, even under the microscope. If anything, they seemed to be the healthiest part of the plant. Marigold sighed, wiping her hands on her jeans. She didn't like not being able to work something out. But then again, she wasn't at the giving up stage just yet.

"I guess you've asked a lot of succulent experts about this," Marigold said. "If it was as simple as whether you'd been giving them enough water they'd probably have worked it out. So I'm guessing it's something interacting with the magic somehow. Have you changed anything with the potions you've been using?"

"Not really. I mean, I tried a couple of new ones a month ago, but this is all more recent. And some of these have had far more in the way of potions than others, but there's no correlation between that and how sick they are. "

"Hmm. Is there any way you can contact any of your buyers and see how their plants are doing?"

Laurel perked up at the idea. "I'll message Sorrell. I gave them one to give them good focus for studying. Let me message them."

A few moments later, and Laurel turned her phone round to show Marigold. The succulent in the picture was healthy, green, growing well, with thick leaves.

"It's something at my fucking flat," Laurel said. "I'm so tired of that place. I have to spend so much energy just holding back the mould. Fucking landlords, fucking piece of shit landlords..." and Laurel dissolved into tears. "I'm sorry," she said, as Marigold put her arms round her. "It's just really stressing me out. I thought I was getting everything sorted but I'm useless, I'm useless like I always am."

"You're the last person I would call useless," Marigold said, but though she meant it, she couldn't conjure up her usual optimistic tone. Maybe the start of the semester was getting to them both. Marigold was at least as stressed out on Laurel's behalf than she was on her own. It had taken Laurel years to get the courage to get back to study, and Marigold had thought it was going okay. They had talked about it at the weekend, it had sounded like Laurel had a lot of work to do, yes, but none of the bleakness and stress she had previously been facing.

Now Marigold wasn't so sure. Everything hinged on Laurel's witchcraft, on her business success, her whole plans for the year. But her newfound focus was so hard-won and still so fragile, it was almost as if she'd set herself up to fail. Marigold was trying to pick Laurel up, but she was feeling the looming anxiety of failure approach herself as well.

"Hey," Marigold said, forcing up her optimism. "We're going to fix this, okay? This is a business set-back and you expect to have those. Everyone does. It just so happens that yours are more magical than other people's, so they don't have easy solutions laid out in how-to-do-business guides.

Which is a relief in a way, because it means you have to bring them to me and I'm *much* more interesting than any how to do business guide.

Laurel managed a smile. Which was all Marigold wanted really.

They picked themselves up, and together they had another look. If the answers weren't here, they'd find them somewhere else. Marigold had confidence in her microscopes though–they were, if not people or friends, at least like pets. They weren't as powerful as the ones she had access to at the research institute, but they did always feel like they were on her side.

And she suspected it wasn't the level of magnification that was the issue here.

"Laurel," she said, thinking. "Do you know any spell that could make something magic show up here, if that's what's going on?"

Laurel thought for a moment, and Marigold couldn't help but grin at that face, deep in thought, her blue hair falling over her defined face.

"I can try a simple incantation that might work," she says. "It won't change what's there, but it might make it more perceptible to us. Otherwise... yes, but it would be a potion and would take me an hour or two."

"May as well give the incantation a try," Marigold said and perched on a stool as Laurel got out her phone and started typing.

"Will be better if we say it together... just trying to remember it all."

When she was done, she showed it to Marigold and the two of them read it together out loud:

We stand together, we stand alonein hope the hidden will be shownSo let the truth be brought to lightreveal the magic to our sight.

Once, Marigold would have felt self-conscious doing something like this, but her voice and Laurel's harmonised oddly well, and she felt some of its power. Toad - her frog familiar - stirred in her pocket and then settled down. Of course: she was a witch now.

Marigold returned to the microscope and looked carefully at the sample. At first, she didn't see anything different, and then she did, so clearly. She yelped.

"Wait what?" Laurel asked, standing behind her.

"I saw something move!"

"What where?"

Marigold returned her eyes to the microscope, seeing tiny black squares moving–no, running, wriggling even–out of the sample.

"There... and there... oh shit they're everywhere!"

Marigold could feel her adrenaline levels shooting up, each of them hyping the other up in part excitement at having potentially found the cause of the problem, and part fear. Marigold was used to bugs - she'd go hunting for magic ones as needed - but there was something about the idea of an infestation, about them going haywire all around them, that put her into panic mode.

The whole microscopic thing wasn't ideal either. And she didn't want to harm them–especially that, as they were magic, she couldn't guarantee they didn't have feelings. She looked through the microscope again. They showed no signs of escaping–fortunately, they were all still near the plant. Marigold thought quickly, grabbed a petri dish and with the ends of tweezers ushered them in and clicked on the lid.

They weren't quite microscopic, exactly. They were just on the edge of being seen by the naked eye, tiny specs moving ever so slightly, but with no detail visible. There was no way either of them could have spotted them on the plants, or have distinguished them from specs of soil.

Marigold guided Laurel up to the microscope and let her take a look at the bugs in the petri dish.

"Ah fuck," Laurel said, looking even more despondent than she had when she first reported the problems with her plants.

"It really looks like you might have an infestation," Marigold said. "I'm sorry."

Laurel and Marigold spent Saturday cleaning as best they could. They repotted the succulents, washing soil off their roots. They cleaned the area they'd been in and placed the pots in plastic trays.

Marigold knew right from the start that it wasn't going to be as simple as this, but maybe it would at least reduce the amount of infestation, buy them some time.

"Stay tonight?" Laurel said, already yawning. "I've got Charlotte - you know my friend Charlotte from uni? - coming for brunch tomorrow, and you should join us."

Marigold nodded. "I'll just check in on some emails and stuff," she said, as Laurel offered to heat up some soup.

"God we're old," Marigold blurted out, as they both laughed. "Soup it is."

Laurel fell asleep almost immediately and Marigold said goodnight to Alfred, the monster under the floor, and then intertwined herself in her girlfriend's limbs contentedly. Of course there were setbacks, but right now, warm and comfortable, she knew that as long as they were together things would be okay.

She was woken by Laurel pulling open the curtain–it wasn't direct sun here, so much as a sort of murky light, but enough to signify it was morning. Mid, encroaching on late morning even, the perfect time for brunch.

Connor had salvaged a waffle maker from god knows where, and though Laurel had complained and sanitised it three times and scrubbed it with bleach before being confident enough to eat anything made using it, she had to confess that it was nice to have a waffle maker. Charlotte arrived while it was heating with fresh fruit and cream. Leilani already had plans (other brunch–it was a Wellington Sunday after all) but it looked like there'd be plenty of waffles if she came home still hungry.

Connor went to the dairy to get maple syrup–well, maple sauce, given their budgets, but it was close enough. With a few other ingredients retrieved from the cupboards, including some homemade jam, they had pretty much everything they needed. The dining table was too small, so she'd set it up on the larger coffee table in the living room.

With everyone back, she brought through the food, made waffles and everyone helped themselves piling up fruit and cream–and, in Connors case, bacon bits from a cardboard box. Everyone else declined his offer to share them.

"I thought you only ate animals you killed yourself?" asked Marigold.

"Oh, these are vegan," Connor responded confidently. "Also. How do you know whether I do or don't spend my time killing pigs?"

"Give it here," Marigold said, reaching for the packet. She read the ingredients aloud. "Vegan bacon bits. Who would have thought?"

She curiously tapped the box until one fell on her hand and sampled it, chewy and savoury.

"Verdict?" Connor asked as she handed the box back.

"Better than I would have thought, but I'll stick with what I've got thanks."

Marigold had plenty of fruit all arranged in separate piles on the waffles which she cut accordingly. It was good food; even though she was a baker herself she liked it when Laurel made food for her.

Connor reached over and grabbed some envelopes.

"Oh before I forget, we have mail for a Mildred Windflower. Laurel, I assume that's some relative of yours and not a true name."

Marigold half choked on a waffle. Mildred may be a well-established name associated with witches, but it was definitely not a name that suited Laurel. Connor–being Connor–saw the humorous potential in the moment and ran with it.

"Laurel's her middle name you see, and..."

Laurel rolled her eyes. "Yeah, I'm taking care of it."

"Who's Mildred?" Marigold asked. "Did I meet her at Christmas?"

"No, not yet. But you will. It's My Aunt Mildred–you know the fibre witch?"

"No," Marigold said. "But I'll add her to my spreadsheet of your family. You have a lot of them."

"Yes, okay, fair. Mildred's a pretty famous fibre artist, for people in those circles anyway. She made the cushions in my room. She's a cousin but I call her an Aunt. She's been overseas for several years and she's coming home, to NZ at least, I'm not sure where she'll be staying yet. But she's using my address while she gets a few things sorted. You'll meet her—I'm sure you'll get on great!"

"I don't know much about textiles," said Marigold, uncertainly.

"Exactly. You're both nerds who are obsessed with something. That means you'll get on far better than you would with someone who was half interested in the same thing as you. Anyway, it will be a few months... wait, do you really have a spreadsheet of my family?"

"Nothing creepy. Just who I've met and the main things you've told me. So if I'm going to meet someone I can refresh my memory... you don't mind, do you?"

"I don't... no, I don't mind. It's just terribly *you*. But I appreciate you care enough."

Marigold shrugged, though she was feeling herself flush. "People who are important to you are important to me."

Laurel reached forward and kissed Marigold, quickly and gently, on the lips, ignoring the others in the room. "That's really lovely of you. I know our family can be a lot sometimes. I'll quiz you on us sometime!"

"Better not!" Marigold said laughing.

Just as Marigold was wiping up the last of the maple sauce on her plate with the remnants of a waffle, they were interrupted by a commotion outside. Laurel moved to look out of the window while Connor headed out of the door. He returned with his arms in the air as if in a gesture of cynical triumph.

"Bus stuck in Devon Street!" he yelled in the air. "Bus gone down Devon Street."

That was enough to make the rest of them stand and move towards the door. Marigold licked her fingers. This was true Wellington excitement, like the time the pub opposite parliament caught fire or the time lightning struck the Wind Wand.

"Why. The Fuck. Would anyone try and drive a bus down Devon Street?"

"Oh, it's an annual occasion for something to get stuck in the bend there."

"Something, yes, but usually a truck. A whole bus. Seriously???"

"Seems so."

"Okay, field trip time, we have got to take a look at this one."

"I wish I had brought my good camera," Marigold mumbled, taking out her cellphone. They headed up the street to where a bus, was, indeed, stuck in the hairpin bend.

"I reckon they're going to have to crane it out," Connor said. "That happened once before, someone told me."

"The rubbish truck?"

"Probably."

Marigold had lived in Wellington long enough to know that pieces of excitement like this were what brought the city together. Flying trampolines, pubs catching fire, and yes, large vehicles getting stuck on Devon Street–they were basically Wellington's Mardi Gras, its sense of excitement and unity, a chance for people to let go together. She wasn't sure what else one could really ask for.

Right now, though, she felt outside of the crowd when she should have felt one with it, sort of at the edge, struggling to fit in. She was still thinking about the succulents, thinking about her study, not sure if things were going to work out.

As the four of them watched, a small crowd gathered, some with coffee in hand, others with cameras. Marigold felt for the driver who was probably cowering behind the far side of the bus with embarrassment, but on the other hand, really, who *would* try and drive a bus down Devon Street.

Marigold walked up to uni from Aro street, using the opportunity to have a good nosy at the bus on the way up. A bus! On Devon street! Once they were past the incident Toad jumped up out of her pocket and onto her shoulder, settling there comfortably, and she stroked his back with a finger, which he seemed to like. She'd seen a couple of secure messages come though about her enquiry about the succulents, but it would be easier to wait until she was at a computer to look at them, and it would be good to get some work done now she'd had a bit of time off.

The boundaries she'd set for herself around weekend work just weren't cutting it any more. She supposed it was only for a time, that she'd done well to get this far, but still, she was feeling herself slipping.

It was a steep hill up but she'd grown up in Wellington, she was used to hills. She rounded the corner and walked across the carpark to her building. She could see the whole city from here, the city and the harbour and the green belt and the hills across the water, and it never got old. She touched the card reader with her fingers–she didn't need her card any more, had access to the whole campus, though she was scared to use it–and headed for the lift.

Back home, though, after going through a new set of literature about antibiotic use, Marigold's thoughts were back with the succulents. She knew she couldn't deal with this alone. This wasn't a natural infestation–or even just a supernatural one. Closer examination had confirmed what Marigold already knew: they were not living creatures but tiny machines, nanobots that had been programmed to act in a particular way. Someone had done this deliberately.

She was wary about saying too much on her mailing lists, or even her encrypted chat app. Whoever did this either knew a lot about the intersections of magic and technology and was involved in both, or at the very least had people working for them who did. Until Marigold knew their motivations, she was uneasy about being on the wrong side of them.

She noted down what she did know: that there were nanobots that infested and killed plants that had been infused with magic. It seemed incredibly specific, and she didn't understand why someone would want to do that–unless they were intended for something else and this was either a side effect or something had gone wrong.

She pulled out a spiral-bound notebook from a drawer, one with big sunflowers on the cover. She'd started it as a kid, noting down her contacts, people who knew about magic. More recently, it had the names of scientists who used magic. There were none into nanotechnology, so far as she was aware, but her flipping through her notebook inevitably landed her on one name. Who knew about both botany and robotics–as well as magic?

Mary-Ann, that was who. Marigold jabbed at the phone number beneath her name. She was going to have to use her least favourite form of technology. She picked up her phone and dialled the number, trying to plan ahead of time what to say, trying to keep calm.

The phone rang for what seemed like a lifetime, propelling her anxiety, before something worse than it being answered happened. Voicemail. Marigold slammed her finger into the red end call button so hard it hurt, swiping it desperately to the centre. She told herself to take deep breaths. She told herself she could do this.

This time when she got voicemail, she was prepared.

Hi this is Marigold Nightfield I'm on 021 000 0000 that's 021 000 0000. I've found something magical and quite urgent that I could really use your expertise on. If you could call me back I'd appreciate it thank you.

Marigold hung up and glared at her phone. She wouldn't have minded if Mary-Ann struggled with technology or even if she'd just never got round to using it. But that wasn't the case—she was a retired Professor of Engineering specialising in robotics, for heaven's sake. But when she was working she viewed email as an imposition, butting heads with various senior figures by arguing that the fact it wasn't in her contract when she was first employed meant it was unreasonable to require it of her now.

Marigold would not have liked to have been on the wrong side of her, that's for sure. But fortunately the two of them had always got along, despite the fact Mary-Ann had insisted even in retirement that email was *still* an unreasonable imposition and refused to have anything to do with it.

Marigold's phone buzzed in her hand, and she panicked trying to remember how to answer a call, pressing the green symbol frantically before the arrow showed her she had to drag it. If Mary-Ann could see this she'd laugh her head off, pointing out that she wasn't the one who was bad with technology.

Perish the thought.

"Sorry I left my phone while I was out gardening. I hope I didn't leave you hanging too long. How are you? And your father's back in the country by now–I must get in touch with him."

Marigold managed to murmur some niceties, enquire after Mary-Ann's wellbeing, and get to outlining the situation without very much interruption.

"And you're sure they're nanobots not some, I don't know, cursed beetle or something?"

Marigold privately thought cursed beetles would be easier to deal with, but she did not express that thought.

"No, I looked under the microscope. They're not organic - at least not primarily organic - they have square edges and corners and there seems to be some sort of processor as well. This is just under my microscope at home–I didn't want to risk taking them into the lab."

"Wise. Very wise. Right. So I can't tell you what these are, but I think I can give you a couple of leads. Firstly, constructing nanobots isn't something just anyone can do–not even just anyone with magic or know-how. I can't tell you who is ultimately responsible for these, but I would place money on who got them made. Here's a name for you: Clayton Simm. He's one of those who takes money, produces the item, and doesn't ask too many questions. Sometimes he outsources the project–and I know nanoro-botics is something he's done before."

"Is he a witch?"

"Thankfully not–we don't need people like that damaging our already stellar reputations. But he's definitely aware of magic, and may even have dabbled in the basics himself."

"Good to know. Sounds like a fun guy."

"He's not malicious. Just... mercenary..."

Marigold jotted down some more details and chatted a little more to Mary-Ann before ending the call. She felt drained–she did every time she had to talk on the phone. And she liked talking to people, even though she was often kinda awkward at it–but something about the phone-based medium just destroyed her.

She had more enquiries to make, but thankfully the next two on her list were capable of using email, or in this case the encrypted messaging system scientists interested in magic often preferred. One did actually have research interests in nanorobotics, though more specifically in the healthcare system–the other didn't but was both a botanist and an engineer and particularly renowned for having a wide-ranging knowledge. She didn't expect to hear from him immediately, but the first, despite him being on the east coast of the US which meant by Marigold's reckoning it was late at night, got back to her in the chat function pretty much immediately.

Unsurprisingly, he wanted to know more, and for the first time in her life, Marigold found herself hesitant to give out too many details. Oh, she was used to hiding magic and witchcraft - or, if not hiding them exactly, at least talking about them in a way that ensured she wouldn't be taken too seriously - but these were her people! Magical scientists and witches with an interest in science. But this time one of them was most likely the cause of the problem. And with their motivation unclear, she had to be more than a little careful.

She told him what she felt comfortable with, cautiously, thinking he only wanted to get a better sense of the problem—well, that and curiosity. She would be curious in the same position. In return, she got some answers. Not final ones, but a few leads on experiments with magic and nanotechnology that didn't lead to fully published papers or even write-ups for those in the know, and a couple of names.

Two of the people she'd contacted had both mentioned one name. Thomas MacUspaig, last seen in Wellington. May or may not still be alive—in his words, he was "getting on a bit". A specifically local lead. It was unlikely to be a coincidence.

Marigold opened messenger and passed the name on to Laurel.

>> People think this guy might be connected. Wellington-based, may or may not still be alive. Any chance you can dig through your databases and stuff?

>> Onto it!

>> Thanks. You're so good at this stuff.

>> Don't thank me! You're doing all this for my benefit.

>> Nah. It's for our future success. I can live a life of luxury while you make a killing in the succulent industry.

>> Yeah, I can totally see you hanging out doing nothing. Very like you. Let me get back to you on Thomas.

Marigold sent a small torrent of emojis in response and headed upstairs to refill her coffee. It was time to get to work on some experiments of her own, much more comfortable than talking to people.

Finding the cause of a problem should lead to a solution, but it turned out to not be that simple. Marigold liked being able to fix things, but she was out of her depth here. These creatures weren't ones that could be handled by traditional pest control methods. She didn't like the idea of that anyway: tiny robots - even problem-causing tiny robots - set off her natural protective instincts. But at least she could use the ideas as a starting point.

Two ideas from what she read did seem like they had some potential: to add something the pests didn't like to avert them and to provide them with a nearby environment that was more pleasant for them to attract them away from where they were causing trouble. Marigold laughed, imagining creating a resort environment for tiny robots. That would be delightful! But this was a serious problem, and it would take some experimentation to work out what they were attracted and averse to.

Thanks to Laurel, Marigold had more google-fu than she used to when it came to googling witchy stuff. She knew what terminology actual witches were more likely to use and how to filter out other understandings of witchcraft. But despite that, *magic bugs* as a search term starting point didn't get her very far. Nor did *magical infestation*–or at least it went down the route of something that seemed to be close to possession which was very dark and probably fictional stuff and unnerved Marigold more than she could justify.

She thought for a bit. They were not insects, but she knew some people were less precise than her - knew it and it annoyed the fuck out of her - so she tried it anyway. And at last, she got somewhere. Magic fleas. "Are you kidding?" she said aloud. Actual magic fleas. And then she found this idea they had become their own population, bred from the fleas of familiars. Well.

Marigold reached into her pocket to stroke her frog familiar and was so relieved she hadn't got a cat or anything that could carry fleas. She made a mental note to check with Laurel that Tibbs was up to date with his flea meds.

Anyway. Magic fleas evolved on familiars? Marigold was sure genetics didn't work like that, and while she was no expert in magic, she was reasonably sure magic didn't work like that either. But at least someone else had seen microscopic creatures like this before. It was a good sign. She kept searching. And she found something.

They weren't the same and they weren't the same plant–these were creatures on roses, destroying a prized collection, causing it to wilt. Again, they were borderline microscopic and could only be seen because this person was a botanist and wanted to investigate what was happening to their roses in more detail. And though the creatures weren't identical, Marigold could see the exact same magic signature, the effect they were having on water intake and other substances around them.

If she'd hoped for an easy solution to be included in the article, well, that would just be too simple. But there were some detailed descriptions of the bots and some theorising about what they might have been and where they might have come from. It was a good start and at least gave Marigold some starting points in what to find out. She made a few notes for herself on her tablet, and then she checked her herb garden. It still looked healthy.

Which supported her theory that these particular nanobots were targeting magic-infused plants. Considering the destruction she had seen at Otari-Wilton's, that meant someone had been infusing some of the plants there as well. She wondered if whoever that was was the real target.

She was struggling with the whole thing though. There was a bigger picture to all of this, something she couldn't get her head around just by looking down a microscope. Working out this problem - and a way to solve it - might start here in this lab, but it was going to require understanding people and interactions and motivations, not just what became clear at the other end of a microscope. And that...

that was more difficult. She wanted to be able to solve it with Laurel, but sometimes she worked best alone and it seemed like this was going to be one of those sometimes.

Marigold swung round on her stool. She pressed her hands together and then drew them apart in a way that allowed the illusion of glittering threads to hang between them. With perfect focus, she could bring her arms out wide without a single one of them breaking. She'd been working on simple tricks like this in the short amount of time since she had become a witch. They weren't just ends in themselves but helped her develop the mindset and access to parts of her thinking that allowed her to do more complicated witchcraft.

But she was, before everything else, a researcher. There were research witches - that wasn't a contradiction in terms - but she still wondered if by doing what she loved she was wasting the small amount of time she had with the ability to do magic.

The next day, she was back on campus, with more in her calendar than she liked. In between, she hung out in the shared study space, and in various small nooks around campus, booting up the encrypted messaging system she used, factored in TFA on a dongle thing on her key chain - she didn't like doing it on her phone - and read through the messages.

Marigold - this time on a couch in a corner by a window, just behind one of the cafes - laughed to herself about how many people with no particular knowledge of her question had done extensive searching for her. This community was full of people who liked diving into research rabbit holes. It was also full of people who were looking for an excuse to distract themselves from their own research or, worse, their own grant applications. She skim-read the abstracts of the articles so she knew what she was dealing with, and saved the citations for looking at later while she moved on to the more specific messages.

Two of the messages suggested contacts but didn't offer much more information. Those were potentially helpful, but difficult. Marigold was always up for approaching people cold to ask about science, but she needed to know whether they were fully immersed in the magic community, had no awareness, or had absolutely no idea. Otherwise, it was very easy for her to put a foot wrong, and completely destroy all hopes of getting anywhere with the lead at best–and put both her own reputation and the privacy of magic users at risk at worst.

The email that held the most immediately useful information was dense and technical. Marigold saved it for after the lab she was teaching, and took her phone outside to read it, sitting on the grass in the cemetery that adjoined the university, high on the hill.

It summarised a couple of attempts at dealing with magic-infused nanotechnology and referenced a few experiments, all of which seemed to have been building off the others. The reason for showing this, the author explained, was that it was quite likely these either came from or were in part copied from these experiments in some way–no-one had seen the need to reinvent the wheel, so to speak. And if *that* was true, they would all emit the same signature.

Marigold grasped the significance of this immediately. There was a way to detect the presence of nanobots. If she was going to test something - like an antidote - she needed a way to see if it was working and prove that. An independent verification. It wasn't a solution but it was a step in the right direction.

It was time for Marigold to call in some favours. She finished her bottle of iced tea.

People thought she was bad at networking. *She* thought she was bad at networking, but there was one type she could do well. She could be enthusiastic about other people's things as well as her own, and–sometimes the ways people found it endearing was a bit patronising, but often they genuinely appreciated it, and it was useful nonetheless.

She began her search in the physics department, cornering a grad student she knew mostly from shared events with pizza.

"If you wanted to pick up a particular frequency in the range of..." she asked, and quickly noted down an answer.

She found another ally in the engineering department. "How would you display and output..." she asked the red-haired young woman.

At the bookshop she leaned against the counter, looking cheery. "Do you have any of those small plastic boxes left? The type those branded pens come in–yes those! May I recycle one?"

Then she headed down some outside steps to one of the less used areas of campus and found more confidence than she felt.

"Can I use this space to do something–it will only take five minutes?" she asked, looking as innocent as possible, at the door to the maintenance area. "We're not allowed to use them in the biology labs and I *definitely* don't want to risk a call out. I think the fire service charge a fee for excessive..."

Whether the facilities management person was *actually* convinced by her fire alarm argument, or just didn't have the energy to care, Marigold, with an old Raspberry pi, and a collection of other components she'd been donated, put together the detector quite simply. Now it was just programming it–because it wasn't a matter of just detecting a frequency, but a pattern thereof. And she knew where to go for that.

"Morning," she said, having snuck past reception to the CompSci department. The older man turned slowly in his chair, away from his three-monitor setup.

"Marigold. How are you?"

Marigold skipped the niceties, passing over her laptop. "So my code's mostly right, but there's a bit here..."

She'd taken some of his classes in first year and he had tried to persuade her to switch majors. She hadn't, but that hadn't meant they didn't enjoy catching up now and again. And he was always happy to help her out with things like this. He knew something was going on but didn't ask too many questions.

And now, with a few tweaks, she had a fully functional plant-destroying-nanobot detector.

Progress was being made.

Once again, Marigold was back in Otari-Wilton's Bush, on her hands and knees, hunting for something between the trees. She was there alone - she didn't want to tell Laurel until she had something tangible, didn't want to get her hopes up - but she still wished she had some help.

The detector was mostly not magic, but there was a hint of it in there as well. And, well, either it was playing up or Otari-Wilton's Bush was absolutely crawling with these parasites. Absolutely crawling with them. They were everywhere.

Which was one hell of a discovery.

Marigold crawled backwards to the path and dusted down her jeans, well aware she might be dusting off nanobots as well as just soil and leaves and the odd insect this time. She came to the conclusion that either Laurel had picked the bots up here when meeting her for lunch, or these things really were everywhere. Like, out in the entire world everywhere. She wasn't sure which option she liked least if she was honest.

She walked home, trying out the detector on grass verges and plants as she went. They weren't *quite* everywhere, admittedly, but they definitely weren't confined to one location. This felt bigger than anything Marigold had dealt with before–bigger than moving around the world as a kid, bigger than starting her PhD research, bigger than talking to monsters even. She felt rather out of her depth. And it wasn't that she had a lack of people to turn to - she had Laurel, she had her father, she had friends, she had colleagues - so much as she didn't know who would be best to talk to about this. It felt rather like something else she had to take on entirely alone.

She reached her home and paused. Her grandmother's herb garden - now her herb garden, she supposed, but it would always feel like her grandmother's - was laid out at the front, with square beds and little white gravel tracks between them. Marigold swallowed. She actually didn't want to know if it was infested. She didn't think the plants were infused with magic, but they had been used by magical people for so long it wasn't clear. Laurel's succulents had been destroyed pretty quickly and badly. The affected plants at Otari-Wilton's had also looked in a bad way, but she assumed magic had been worked on them also. She imagined she wasn't the only witch who was drawn to the place.

The scientist part of her said she wanted to have all the information she could get. But the part of her that had put years and years into maintaining this garden, into keeping it neat, ensuring that even the least hardy herbs thrived and that the more resilient ones - the mints and the parsleys - were cut back and didn't take over, raking the gravel, sending samples of the less common plants to her grandmother's friends and network as needed... just didn't want to know. When she was in Dunedin she had worried about this garden more than anything else, and if it was now under threat, she didn't think she could handle it.

She chose the easy option: she delayed making a decision. Rather than heading through the front door she went down to her lab and sat with the detector on her lap. She had no idea where to go from here.

Marigold taught three tutorials in a row the next morning, two of them favours called in in exchange for her asking others to cover for her. She had too much going on and she'd shot herself in the foot a little asking for favours that needed to be paid back later, trading short term alleviation of her issues for just making them even more unmanageable down the track.

But two of them were for first years, and it was just late enough in the year for them to be opening up and getting comfortable speaking in monosyllables, but early enough that they were still enthused, hadn't been overwhelmed by housing dramas or financial dramas, or whatever else seems manageable early on but accumulated to get the better of so many of them by second year. It was a satisfying point to be teaching them.

She'd found teaching scary at first, but she did enjoy it. Just not three classes in a row.

She walked home after that, eating leftover homemade pizza on the way. She forced herself to do an hour of writing before anything else. Then, in desperate need of something to do with her hands and not her brain, she set to work finishing clearing out the semi self-contained unit of the house that had been where her grandmother lived. It had been a while since she'd even been in and she paused as she turned the light on, and let herself look around the room for anything that still needed to be done. She was surprised to find herself hit by a wave of sadness that overwhelmed all the practical intentions she'd begun with.

She had told herself that her grandmother was old, she had been ill, she had known her death was coming and was quite philosophical about it, but sometimes... sometimes she just missed her. Marigold sat on the bed. Last time they had been in here her and Laurel had found a metal object with the powers of a witch inside, hidden by Marigold's grandmother. She hoped there weren't any more weird secrets lurking.

Most of her grandmother's things had been gone through and sold or donated. Marigold dragged the cabinet that showcased her metalwork through to the living room. That wasn't getting rid of things; it was putting her grandmother's talent on full display in the main room, where it deserved to be. Clearing out the last few things though, Marigold was less sure. She felt silly; they'd had visitors stay in this room after all, it had hardly been kept as a shrine. But she couldn't help but feel it seemed like she was trying to erase the last traces of her grandmother's presence. It didn't matter that the opposite was true; it still made her feel uncomfortable.

It wasn't going to get any easier if she left it, though, and so she sorted through the last items, packed away some stuff to keep, made a pile to donate for her father to look through first. The place didn't need re-decorating - it was neutral enough - but she'd want to swap the furniture around, make her childhood bedroom into a spare room, and maybe get some cushions and stuff to give it a new look. She'd probably only use the kitchenette for coffee and noodles or reheating stuff, so the existing utensils and crockery there were fine, and she already had her own bathroom products that would just need moving - her father had an en-suite so the main bathroom was essentially hers anyway. The bed was better than hers, though, so she'd keep that and get a new duvet cover that was more her style because this was a queen and her current one was a double–but all the rest of the linen could be re-used.

It was actually surprising she hadn't done this earlier–but there had been no need for her own space when she was the only one living in the house, and before that she had been in Dunedin, and before *that* it was too close to her grandmother's death to even be thinking about.

Now seemed the right time though. She'd checked with her father not because she needed his permission for things to do with the house - they were trialling being housemates in a way that meant they could both make decisions - but because Marigold's grandmother was, after all, his mother and she knew he might have feelings about the place. But being overseas for a year seemed to have given him the sense of distance that he needed to be okay with it–either way, he just said not to throw out anything she'd made without checking with him. He hadn't offered to help which in other circumstances she might have found annoying but this particular time it felt satisfying for her to just get on with it.

She found it wasn't as difficult as she'd expected it to be, and the more she cleaned out the space and made it look like just any self-contained unit, the easier it was. Maybe as well as cleaning up the dust she was removing the last vestiges of magic...

Her train of thought was interrupted by a knock at the door.

"One moment," she yelled, expecting a courier package. She put the sheets in the basket and ran through the house to the front door, swinging it open. And then she stopped. The young woman at the door had shorter hair than the last time she saw her, which meant it took extra time for Marigold to process her face, but only a second.

"Memory!" Marigold yelled, flinging herself into her best friend's arms. "What the hell are you doing in town?"

Marigold and Memory had been best friends since they were sixteen. Marigold had returned to school after two years doing correspondence school from Japan, and Memory's family had just moved back from Australia. Aside from their return to school and Wellington after years away, they hadn't been the obvious pair; Marigold was all about science while Memory spent every moment she could in the art rooms. Marigold talked to everyone she could and frequently put her foot in it, while Memory was reserved, her words chosen carefully.

"Taking a pack of kids round the City Gallery and Te Papa. I didn't want to tell you because I didn't think I'd get chance to see you, but I made a deal with one of the parent helpers and cut and run for it. I only have an hour or so. I, uh, did text you."

Marigold looked round for her phone.

"Shit. Sorry."

"No worries. I expected no less. I'm just glad you were home. It's been *months*."

Memory lived in Whanganui, teaching high school art and - hilariously in Marigold's view, home economics - and loved it, but despite being less than three hours drive away their paths didn't cross as often as they would have liked.

Both of them found themselves endlessly busy; neither were particularly good at making plans.

"Come in, come in. How are you? What's new?"

Memory spun around on her foot to reveal a wide but slightly nervous smile.

"Pregnant, for starters."

Marigold stopped still at the entrance to the living area, only just managed to avoid gasping.

"No way. But... but you're my age! That's way too young to have a baby."

"Ha! No seriously, I'm ready, Troy's ready, may as well make a start. It's not public, though, not just yet."

"I need to make us something to toast this... one mo ment..." Marigold ran outside and came in with leaves of mint and lemongrass and a few berries, then used a wooden spoon to knock down a cocktail shaker from a high shelf which she caught, awkwardly, with one hand.

"I can't..."

"I know you can't drink. I'm gay and a nerd but I'm not completely clueless about the ways of normal people. This is just a mocktail, it has lemongrass for strength and nurturing and ginger to prevent nausea. Oh and plenty of sugar so it actually tastes good."

Marigold filled up the shaker from icemaker on the front of the fridge and shook it hard, pouring into proper cocktail glasses.

"To your little one," Marigold said.

"To your goddaughter," Memory said, and Marigold put a hand over her mouth to suppress a squeal. "I mean if you'll accept. Troy's parents are very into the whole getting the kid baptised thing, and you're the person I most want to be looking out for my kid, and I feel having a witch as a god-mother is just the right amount of quiet subversiveness..."

"No curses, I promise."

"No. I know you're not that sort of... well you're actually a witch now. It's weird, when we were kids I thought that was just your quirk, but now I find magic increasingly interesting. Can you send me some book recs? There's so much weird shit out there I don't know where to start."

"Book recs are my thing!" Marigold responded. "Of course. And there are bits you can do yourself, even without any magic in your heritage."

As she'd said, Memory could stay only an hour, and Marigold found herself energised and delighted to see her, but even that intense hour or so left her exhausted. She hated that it was like this—she wasn't shy, wasn't even an introvert as most people understood it, she was innately social, loved spending time with people, it just... took so much out of her.

She sat down at the computer to play some simple mindless games and try and restore her energy but before she did a message from Laurel caught her eye. A lead on Thomas MacUspaig, with an address. A local address.

Things were really all happening today.

Laurel and Marigold caught the bus from Kelburn across to Newtown–the other side of town, but not too far away. They swiped empty cardholders as they got on and off–being able to mimic microchips with magic was Marigold's discovery, and they hadn't used it for anything terribly untoward, but it had saved them quite a bit in bus fares.

They hadn't been able to find email and the only phone number they came across was disconnected–but the person in question was a shareholder in a small consulting LLC and had given a residential address on the companies register. Laurel was good at researching these things–Marigold wouldn't have had a clue where to start. The address was a few years old and the business had since wound up, but it was the best chance they had of finding out what was going on.

The address took them to a narrow, two-storey villa in a street crammed with them. Most of them had definitely seen better days, though a few were freshly painted and had neat gardens in front. In other words, Marigold suspected, most were owned by landlords who cared only about the rent and little about the upkeep. The house they were looking for was in worse condition than most, but the wide-open door and windows, and the presence of tools in the front garden, indicated that was at least in the process of changing.

There was a little garden at the front but no gate. Marigold and Laurel looked at each other and nodded.

Marigold knocked on the open door. They heard the sound of footsteps, and then a man, probably in his forties, answered.

"Hi," Marigold said and swallowed. "We're looking for a Thomas MacUspaig. Does he still live here?"

"You're about two years too late, I'm afraid," he said. "He's been gone a while."

"Oh." Marigold swallowed. Talking to strangers like this was bad enough, but when something set it off course she struggled. Especially when it was something like death where there were all these unwritten rules you had to follow about it. "I'm sorry," she said.

"Don't be. He lived to a hundred and two, still in his own home, old enough to meet three great-grandchildren. We should all be so lucky. Sorry, I'm his grandson, people call me Tay. Please come in. Watch your step–it's a bit of a mess round here."

Marigold and Laurel shook hands and introduced themselves. The house was indeed a work in progress. The walls were stripped but not sanded, with one sheet of plasterboard missing and waiting to be replaced, the floorboards bare but unvarnished. Marigold stepped gingerly, with Laurel behind, but despite everything, the floor beneath them seemed stable enough. Tay dragged a couple of chairs through from somewhere and perched on a workbench.

"So, you'll be another wanting to know more about his inventions. It's ironic–he never heard much from people while he was alive, but he wanted what he did to be known. Which is why I'm happy to answer questions–it's what he'd have wanted."

Marigold took her cue. This wasn't at all how she had anticipated things would go, but Tay being much more open to talking than she had expected was not a bad thing.

She just had to find a way to play things right, put away what she had been planning to say about the problems with his work and the urgency of resolving the situation, and focus on his wish to share knowledge of his grandfather's work.

"Yes. Thanks for inviting us in. I'm Marigold–I'm a PhD student in biology up at Vic, and this is Laurel who owns a plant development and retail businesses." Marigold liked how Laurel smiled when she introduced her that way. She continued. "We've come across some nanobots on plants that Laurel was working with, and we want to understand what's going on with how they're affecting the plants. I asked around and a couple of people suggested your grand-father might know about them. Do you have any idea about those?"

Tay frowned. "Nanobots? Like those things that are too small to see but can crawl round your veins?"

"Maybe that part is still in the future, but yes, essentially."

"Wow, I don't know. Everything I saw him make was kind of the opposite. Big, mechanical. But honestly, my wife's been going through his notes. She's the scientist–well, the tech person at least. She'd be able to tell you better than me..." He stood and popped his head around what seemed to be the door to the next room.

"Hey, Aishah, could you come through a minute."

The woman who came through was dressed for DIY, in a baggy t-shirt and trackpants, both dusty and with evidence of paint stains. Her hair was the most noticeable thing about her though—solid black, streaked with bright pink. Marigold knew from Laurel that coloured hair took quite a bit of upkeep, and she imagined that, despite her willingness to get on with the messy work, it was something of a priority to this woman.

"Hello," she said warmly. "I'm Aishah."

Before either of them could respond with the introductions, Laurel nudged Marigold, hard, and Marigold looked again at the woman, flinching as she flickered through eye contact. She recognised the pink streaks in her hair, if nothing else, the contrast with the darkness of her natural colour. This was the same woman they'd randomly noticed that night after the theatre. The woman whose child had magic.

Marigold stepped carefully over the tiles, as Aishah led them through a house in various stages of renovation.

The kitchen stood out in particular–the stove might have been replaced in the last half-century, but she wasn't sure anything else had. Through the back door there was just enough space for a clothesline in a walled garden, and then a workshop about the size of a double garage–it might even have been a garage once, though it wasn't clear how you'd get a car to it.

"Everything in the house Tay either got rid of, sold, or split between his sisters. I know things look bad at the moment but there was some beautiful wooden furniture in here. But the workshop, well, that's proving to be a task in itself. You'll see why."

Aishah pushed open the door which sounded like it didn't really want to be opened, and flicked on a camping lantern. Part of the garage was already illuminated by a shaft of light coming in through the window, but the lantern cast shadows around the rest. Marigold shuffled her way in so Laurel could get in too.

The place was packed.

Marigold and Laurel had both grown up in witching families. Marigold's father's architectural minimalism was an exception - and probably a reaction - against a well-known tendency of witches: they like to accumulate *stuff*. Even by those standards, though, this place was stacked. Boxes and boxes overflowing with papers. Handwritten notes and diagrams scrawled on everything. Shelves filled with wires and other contraptions, while still more seemed to hang from the ceiling. The bench space was thick with dust and tools–and even Marigold couldn't hazard a guess at what most of them would be used for.

"My father-in-law was a very clever man. That does not always go hand in hand with organisation. Here is the proof. Now I've been through and indexed about a third of this, and... well I only know about nanotechnology from TV, but there was nothing that seemed to even relate to it. It's quite modern science, isn't it? So I think your best bet is probably starting over here. I'm sorry, he never did learn to type."

She pulled out a couple of boxes. "I'll get you two some water."

As soon as she'd left, Marigold and Laurel turned to look at each other with open mouths.

"It's not that I'm complaining," Laurel said, in a loud whisper. "Research is good. But I didn't expect..."

"Do you think she knows," Marigold asked, starting to leaf through the large wads of paper. "About the magic, I mean?"

"Well if he was documenting it..." Laurel began, but then Aishah was back at the door with two mugs of water and a plate of TimTams.

"Sorry," she said, indicating the mugs. "We don't have much at this place yet."

"You've been so kind," Marigold said and meant it. "I've started looking through and this guy must have been a genius!"

"Well," said Aishah, smiling. "A man of many ideas at least."

"You have a child, right?" Laurel said, as Marigold pulled out a pile of papers and began to go through them. "I think I've seen you in town."

"It's the hair, isn't it?" Aishah said, grinning.

Laurel ran a hand through her own hair. "It's great hair. Bright colours are the best."

"And yes, just the one. Adam. He's three."

Laurel took a deep breath. It was always hard to approach the topic without either scaring people or making them think you were making things up or, on the converse, being so vague the conversation was pointless.

"Some people in my family, they're born with unusual abilities. When I saw Adam I thought he might..."

"You can say magic," she grinned. "It's in both our lines but neither of our families really talked about it. And yeah, we're trying to teach Adam how to keep a lid on it. But it's like trying to teach them not to swear, you know. The more attention you bring to it the more attractive it becomes."

"Would it help if you knew other parents of children with magical abilities?" Laurel asked. She didn't say witches, not just yet–that could be too much for people. Aishah responded gratefully and Laurel took her email.

"That's part of what's going on here, isn't it?" Aishah asked, and Laurel told her, at last, the full story.

While Laurel kept going through the written papers, Marigold, having tired of reading them, turned on the torch on her phone and started investigating the rest of the workshop. She thought she'd acquired an unholy number of cables in her time, but it turns out she'd barely got started. There were boxes upon boxes of all kinds of electrical components as well, most of which Marigold was not able to put names to beyond the basics like "circuit boards" or "LEDs", tools or mechanical components like gears and switches. Several seemed to be half-finished or trial contraptions as well, but what they might have been used for was anyone's guess. Certainly not Marigold's anyway.

There was nothing that directly said magic nor anything that directly said nanotechnology but Marigold wasn't making any assumptions based on that. This was clearly someone who had fingers in a lot of pies, and it would honestly be more of a surprise if there was something he wasn't interested in.

Marigold's thoughts were interrupted by an excited yelp from Laurel.

"Look what I've found!" she said, pulling out a set of notes that weren't entirely readable, but definitely included the word nanobots.

Marigold caught the bus up to uni and did some work, taking a quick break to have coffee with Neha. Laurel had taken careful pictures of the plans, outside in the sunlight, before putting everything carefully back in the boxes, thanking Aishah and Tay, and then, tired, she'd headed home. Marigold didn't have the focus to take in what they'd found that day, but she did have the brain for data and checking on experiments, work that took her late into the night.

She started the next morning at home–her supervisor had pushed her to submit an abstract for the conference, but writing abstracts was the worst. The only way to get it done was to sit herself at her desk and force herself to do nothing else until it was done. She didn't know why they were so hard - it wasn't like it was long - but somehow typing every word became excruciating for her every time, and it took ridiculously long.

With it done, she rewarded herself by baking and by reading the nanobot plans. She had the plans on her tablet on the kitchen bench side by side with the handwritten gingerbread recipe from her grandmother. Marigold put both her brain and her hands to work. She rubbed butter and flour together, she grated fresh ginger, she measured out golden syrup.

And she wondered why on earth someone would set up nanobots to go after magic plants. It didn't seem to just be plants used in magic - which would cover a lot of them, including most herbs - but plants that had intentionally been given magical properties of their own. That... couldn't happen very often, so to put in such effort seemed like overkill.

The plans didn't exactly mention a motivation, beyond removing magical plants–why he wanted to do so was anybody's guess. There certainly were people who knew about but objected to or disliked magic–some of them thought it was the devil's work, which struck Marigold as pretty silly, and sometimes magic impacted family dynamics which grew resentment. But surely, she thought, if someone hated magic then it would make more sense to go for the plants most *used* in magic.

Marigold finished off the batter. The thing she loved about gingerbread was how the smell permeated the whole house. It was almost, well, a sort of magic. With the gingerbread in the oven, she lay on the sofa to study the plans more carefully, and with it she could pick up the spices: ginger and cinnamon and nutmeg. She'd noticed her senses not being heightened (thankfully, because things were already intense) so much as becoming more precise. What had been a comforting gingerbread smell now had distinct layers and tones that she could pick out.

She'd thought being a witch would be all about having the sort of power to affect things that her grandmother had. She *was* developing some of that, it was true, but far more of it was about less consequential abilities and experiences, changes in the ways she experienced and interpreted the world.

It was no help whatsoever in interpreting the plans. Half the battle was making sense of the handwritten notes—just converting the scribbles to letters in her head. For the rest of it, she had to rely on her ability to put things into a logical sequence and follow them through, slowly and carefully. In doing so, she got a general understanding of how the nanobots worked. Marigold wasn't a hundred per cent sure - because her grandmother certainly didn't tell her every-thing - but she had a pretty good feeling that the fact they only went after magic-infused plants meant her herb garden was safe.

And it explained why Laurel's plants had been affected so badly. She'd been infusing them with specific potions before sale, but all of them had been exposed to a magic solution for nutrition when she first took and began to grow them from a cutting. Being succulents, of course, they retained moisture, so some of that must have lingered in them the whole time, making them vulnerable to the nanobots. That helped her isolate the problem, but the next - and most important, and probably hardest - thing to do was to come up with the solution.

First things first though. The gingerbread had some time to cool on the rack, but while it was still warm she cut herself two thick squares and smothered them with butter which melted into it as soon as they touched. Some things ... some things she would still be able to do when she was no longer a witch, however far away that might be. That was a comfort to her as she pondered how she was going to bring everything together, the new people who were becoming part of her life, and how she was going to fix this problem that was threatening things for Laurel just when things had been looking up. Just when she felt they'd turned a corner.

She was ready for it.

Marigold had a theoretical solution to the plant issue. Putting it into practice was going to be another matter.

She had thought it was going to be something environmental, or some sort of repellent spray—and that might have worked had it been something only affecting Laurel's plants. But it was clear there was a wider issue here—so it was a time for nanobots versus nanobots. A combination of science, engineering, and magic—just what she liked!

She'd make Nanobots to go after the original Nanobots, meaning they could continue the process independently, rather than them having to seek out all the infested areas themselves. She'd worked through the main parts of how they would detect and neutralise the magic killing bots, before spreading out over a wide area to scout for more.

What she didn't feel confident about was how to create them.

She didn't like to be defeated but she was quite sure manufacturing anything other than a prototype nanobot was going to far exceed her abilities–let alone her resources. She was going to have to ask someone for help with this.

And she wasn't exactly happy when she realised who she was going to have to ask for help

She'd tell Laurel when she was sure it was a go–she found talking about work in progress to be hard sometimes, as her brain was still ferreting out possibilities. Everything was so half formulated for Marigold and she was so full of nervous energy that she didn't think she could even articulate it to another person, not even Laurel. No, she needed to continue on the trajectory she was on. It wasn't ideal, but it was the only way she could go forward. It wasn't the first time her brain had been on a trajectory like this, and she knew exactly how it went.

Marigold was interrupted by a text from Laurel–because of course she was.

>>Can you get into town now? Like Uber now?

Marigold laughed at the pun, opening up the Uber app before texting Laurel to check if everything was alright.

>>Yeah, I just need you to see this.

After the Uber navigated the one-way system, the driver dropped her off outside a small café. Laurel was seated outside, with Aishah and her child–Adam.

"Everything okay?" she asked.

"Yeah."

"I'll grab you a coffee while Laurel explains," Aishah said. "What do you drink?"

"Oh, uh. Long black please."

Laurel had already been able to shed some more light on the motivations for the creations of the original nanobots. She'd stayed in touch with Tay and Aishah so she could connect them with members of her family with similar experiences of raising a witch, especially when they had no magic themselves. Carefully, getting their trust, they'd been able to approach it.

"Aishah's confident Thomas wasn't motivated by a hatred of magic," Laurel said, sipping at her tea. "He didn't like its unpredictability in some ways, but that was just why he didn't use it much; he wasn't angry at it or anything. He was probably a witch, but a latent witch, avoiding his own power."

Marigold nodded.

"That fits with the conclusions I've been coming to. And I saw the diary extracts Aishah sent you."

Aishah joined them at that moment, placing a number on the table.

"Thanks for those Aishah," Marigold continued, looking at her. "I mean the diary pages. And the coffee."

"Oh, you're welcome."

The diary extracts *had* shed more light on the situation. Thomas talked about working on botany during his youth, using magic to make some plants stronger. For various reasons the experiments had failed, but he'd known that the principles were sound, and they could develop out of control. Similar concerns to the ones people have about genetic engineering–though not the patenting and priority genome issue, which in Marigold's opinion was the real issue with genetic engineering even though it was so often ignored, there were definitely similarities.

"Okay," Laurel said. "So we were looking more at this diary and... Adam, can you show Marigold what you showed us."

Adam reached forward. Illusions of plants grew from his fingers; strangling plants, pervasive weeds.

"I didn't think I could describe it well," Laurel said.

"It's like an insight into his mindset," Marigold said. "And no, I wanted to see this. You have a powerful kid there. Laurel, your parents are visiting next month right?"

"Already made the connection. They're Facebook friends now."

Marigold watched the plants grow. It was clear now. He was concerned about some plants taking over. So much of the native ecosystem of Aotearoa had already been destroyed already–and there was no telling how much devastation magic could bring.

"That's beautiful, Adam. With that level of power..." Marigold said. "Damn. If only there was some sort of magical training academy."

"There have been a couple," Laurel explained. "But not in New Zealand... oh no, you're having one of your ideas aren't you."

"Just," Marigold said. "I know a teacher, that's all."

"You have a lot of projects..." Aishah observed.

"You're very observant," Laurel replied. "That's Marigold in a nutshell."

Marigold's mind was distracted on the way home.

Thomas wasn't a villain in this–and Marigold wasn't completely sure she was handling things right either. His concerns were very valid–but he seemed to be casting such a broad net.

Most importantly, his work didn't seem to do much for restoring native bush - now a nanobot that killed weasels, *that* would be useful - and it destroyed plants that had magic infused in them for any reason. Yet there was potential, Marigold thought, to infuse native plants with magic to heal them. Certainly, there were some dead native plants at Otari-Wilton's, a reserve and botanic garden that housed only those.

Thomas's approach was very clunky, Marigold thought. And a shame to have been one of the last projects of a man who had a lot of ideas and probably did a lot of interesting stuff. But at least now they appeared to have an answer, it helped them understand how to tackle it–and at least they didn't have to worry about an adversary who was going to fight them when it came to the nanobots.

Marigold poured herself a fresh cup of coffee and put on the pair of blue light filter glasses that still felt a bit weird where they pinched her nose. She placed her laptop on the docking bay where it connected to her two larger screens.

There was plenty of work to be done, and anxious as she was she'd rather have things to occupy her. If she only had a couple of things going on her brain started to wander and overanalyse things and tell her that she needed to feel awkward and embarrassed about every little thing she did.

Nah, she needed to keep busy and life was certainly providing plenty of opportunities for that. She flicked open a document on one screen and a web browser on the other. She turned on some music - what Laurel still called her weird music, which was fair because she *was* weird - and got to work.

Laurel was uncharacteristically late for lunch two days later and looked stressed when she arrived.

"Plants?" Marigold asked, cutting up her panini.

Laurel shook her head.

"No, I mean, yes, those are still an issue, but, flat stuff."

"Connor? Because I've been thinking about..."

"No. Landlord."

"Oh." Marigold's face fell in sympathy. "Bugger."

"Yeah. Putting the rent up immediately, but also talking about either selling or kicking us out so he can renovate."

"And by renovate he means paint over the mould and put the price up forty per cent?"

Laurel rolled her eyes. "Probably. He's going to get a bit of a shock when there's no longer magic holding the mould back. Of course, he'll probably find some way to try and take that out of my bond."

"Ugh. Asshole. We'll fight that if it happens. I thought you had him under control. What happened?"

Laurel stirred her coffee.

"You know I've always been careful about controlling people's minds and consent and stuff."

"I thought that didn't apply to landlords," Marigold said, and Laurel responded with a brief grin.

"Theoretically, I've no problem with using it to push back against landlords given how shit they behave when given free rein, and the unequal power dynamic. But that was when I was only nudging their thoughts in one direction or another—y'know, *maybe this isn't worth putting the rent up*, *sure this looks fine to pass inspection*, that sort of stuff. But now I have more power than that and I haven't quite realised the limits of it. And I don't want to cross the line between persuasion and controlling people. Even when those people are landlords."

"So you've backed off?"

"Yeah. And sort of regret it now but I wouldn't be comfortable with myself if I did go too far. So, maybe I need to be looking at other options now."

"Well..." said Marigold, thinking fast. "I was planning to move into the unit my grandmother had–why not join me? I know it's a bit further from town, but I walk to uni okay, and you'd have privacy, and access to the rest of the house. There's plenty of space for us. I'd need to clear it with my dad but I think he'd be cool. No rent, just power and so on, and it's in good condition. Sunlight even..."

Laurel pondered the idea, twisting her blue hair around a finger.

"Too fast?" Marigold asked. Toad croaked from her pocket and she reached in to give him some attention. He had not yet learned not to interrupt important conversations.

"Yes, no, I'm not sure. Not necessarily but there are so many things. Like, Alfred, I'd need to find someone who was cool with Alfred. And there are the practicalities; like I own this random furniture. And to move in with you and your father–you've already got rules and established ways of doing things, and I don't know if I'm always going to feel like the guest. Oh, you're both great, and I know your dad will be good to me, but I need to feel at home sometimes. And then... well it's not like I could afford even a room this nice, so that would make me feel dependent on you..."

"I'll happily charge you rent," Marigold said, holding out her hand. "Or, y'know, you can contribute in other ways. You have skills we don't. And there's nice bush behind for Tibbs to run round in."

"Yeah..." Laurel sounded uncertain. "I like the idea, and I would really like to live with you, I just don't know if it's the right time or the right place."

"There's no hurry," Marigold said, even though it was killing her not to get an answer right now. "Just think about it, yeah?"

"I will," Laurel said, and the conversation turned to other matters.

But later that night, when she was once again trying to sleep, Marigold turned over the conversation in her head once more, going over each choice of phrase and intonation she had used. Everything Laurel had said had made perfect sense and been entirely reasonable but the thoughts kept hitting her that maybe it was a personal rejection. That she had probably ruined everything by pushing too hard or moving too fast.

She didn't know why she was like this again. The angst of her teenage years had been nicely eclipsed by finding a place for herself, allowing her enthusiasm to come to the fore, to be herself for the first time. She'd got three degrees! She'd lived alone! She'd had relationships, none of which were disasters! She had friends! And things were going well–she was progressing in her PhD and she had a relationship that felt far more solid than her previous ones, with - she dared to hope - long term potential. So why were all her confidence issues, all the criticisms that she'd internalised, coming back now, at the most frustratingly inconvenient time?

Aside from anything else, she simply didn't have time to be dealing with her brain on top of everything else that was going on.

Marigold had one of those mornings when she was dead awake at 6am, and the only thing to do was to get up, slug coffee, throw on clothes after a quick shower, and head to uni before anyone else–except anyone who had pulled overnighters, she supposed. She loved the early mornings, at sunrise, the quiet walk in before the rush hour started, the glinting spiderwebs on fences in the morning sun. She also liked her sleep, but she figured, in these bouts of insomnia which thankfully came less often than they used to, that if she wasn't going to get sleep then she at least needed to compensate herself by making sure she got the most out of the morning.

And so, on this Wednesday morning at not yet six-thirty, her cup filled with coffee, she was walking down through Wilton, and then up through the botanic gardens to uni. She'd been walking through these gardens for years; the rose garden, the steep hills through trees, the observatory at the top, but these past few months she'd been seeing them with new eyes, noticing them with new details. Unlike Otari-Wilton's, these gardens weren't dedicated to native plants, and many of the trees and other plants were non-native. It occurred to her she needed to bring her detector, to see if the nanobots were here as well.

She expected they were. She expected they were scuttling about throughout the whole city right now, drawn to places with a high density of plants, many of them probably working their way through the town belt. Who knew what magic had been worked on the plants there? Who knew how many were at risk?

By the time Marigold arrived, walking through the carpark, there were only a handful of cars and the buses had only just started running. She was out of coffee as well, and would have to either resort to instant or to wait until the cafes opened. But she was, at least, awake, the morning air just cold enough to give her a blast of energy. She hung up her thin summer coat and set herself a word count goal to do before eight when people would start arriving and things would get noisier.

She did well, to start with. She met her goal and was feeling good about her burst of productivity. But as things started getting noisier, she started to feel more unsettled than usual. Her third cup of coffee made her twitchy and anxious rather than energised. She started feeling static build-up in her fingers and when she touched them there were barely visible sparks, unintentional magic feeding off her emotional state. Not ideal. She stood up and stretched, walked a loop around the outside of the building.

She worried about using science and she worried about using magic. She had seen how they had gone wrong and she was, in the scheme of things, relatively new to both, still young, only just a witch. How could she be sure she was on the right path when it had gone wrong for Thomas MacUspaig.

All the good intentions from the start of the day faded. No matter how much she tried to logic herself out of anxiety she couldn't. She ended up sitting there, her laptop plugged into a screen, staring over and over at the data values and getting precisely nowhere.

No-one who had known Marigold before a year ago would ever have believed she'd let a relationship get in the way of her study. Her high school teachers would have laughed out loud at the possibility. And yet here she was.

Laurel hadn't mentioned their conversation about moving. Marigold was taking that to mean she didn't want to, or at least had a lot of reservations and... logically that was fine. Even though her suggestion made sense in many ways there were very good reasons why Laurel wouldn't want to go ahead. They had been together less than a year so it was early days, and if she wanted to wait, or to live together under different circumstances, that all made sense and was totally reasonable and definitely wasn't the death knell of their relationship.

Marigold sucked in a breath. The problem was that, not for the first time, one part of her brain could follow this completely reasonable and balanced way of thinking about a situation, but all the time the other part of her was freaking out or automatically jumping to the worst possible conclusion. And that was exactly what was happening right now.

She was questioning everything. If Laurel had even really liked her in the first place. And yeah, there were good reasons for this level of insecurity, but *come on*. The evidence was very much not matching up with what she was worrying about.

And yet worry she did.

Marigold spent a few minutes after the day's morning lab gulping down yet another cup of coffee and catching up on emails and other bits of work. She was feeling good, mostly–things were coming together. Her main PhD research, which sometimes fell by the wayside against all her magical work, was edging back on track. Today she had got a breakthrough in her results, something new she could write up as an observation and identify as an area for future study, and she was suddenly energised in writing up her thesis again. Finally not finding extracting every word from her brain and typing it into a document excruciating, like draining blood from a stone...

...actually, now she was a witch, blood from a stone was likely easier somehow, and something she should try one day. Anyway. The point was that she was feeling better about things and not like everything was about to fall apart, or like she'd be stuck at this research institute at this university forevermore, growing old while still trying to up her word count. Which was a nice thought, and a bit of a mental reset for her.

After a quick break, she headed back to the office space, determined to keep going with this while her brain was cooperating.

"Magic not working?" Neha said as Marigold poked in her pocket for her swipe card that she hadn't had to use in months.

"What? I just thought my card was in...?"

Neha laughed, gently.

"Marigold, I've seen what you do. Don't worry, I don't think anyone else has caught on. You're some kind of witch, right?"

Marigold sighed.

"You too? Really?"

"Not me. My stepmother's mother–we're not blood relations, so I can't inherit it, but we're family."

Marigold looked round quickly to check no-one was watching, and then encircled the card readers with blue and green sparkles, which faded away into nothing. She turned and grinned at Neha, saying nothing, before sitting down to work.

After lunch, she left her laptop on her desk. The day was overcast but dry enough, and the characteristic Wellington wind caught her as she left the shelter of the building. From here, you could see across the whole city and out to the harbour and Marigold never got tired of it. She turned and walked up a little, heading on to the residential streets, and then down the steep path to the valley below, the wind cool on her scalp below her buzzcut hair.

She hadn't been to Laurel's place as often as she usually would–perhaps because she was having flat difficulties and Marigold didn't want to be adding to the stress more, or perhaps because Marigold was scared to force the discussion about what Laurel would be planning. It felt like no time at all though, as she scooted down the steep steps into the valley in the Autumn sun, and turned through the gate with the paint half-peeled up to the little weatherboard flat on the sunless side of the valley.

It was a cute house. Good potential–if only landlords weren't such jerks who refused to do the appropriate amount of upkeep, and also made people feel bad about mind-controlling them. But even aside from that, with the herb garden mostly in pots at the front, haphazardly laid out, Laurel was using her magic to keep it in as good condition and as close to a decent home as she could. They'd built a lot of their relationship here, and despite feeling a bit weird and anxious about things between them right now, it still had a positive association for Marigold.

But she wasn't here to see this house. She was here to look at the neighbours' places.

And see how likely it was they would have space for a monster.

The first time Marigold had met Laurel had been when she arrived to ask if she could ask Alfred – the monster who lived under her floor - for a tissue sample, which resulted in her hanging upside down through the hole in Laurel's wardrobe to make that request of him. She wondered where else he would be able to live.

She walked round the corner and up and down the street. So many of the old houses seemed to have underfloor space. And more and more people seemed to be comfortable with magic. There had to be *somewhere* he could live happily. He wasn't much trouble, after all.

"Hey, Marigold!" Connor's voice interrupted her thoughts. "Laurel's up at uni."

Marigold stumbled over her words.

"Oh no, I was just. I mean."

"Come in, grab a coffee."

Marigold walked into the house that had started to feel almost like a second home. She perched on a dining chair in the kitchen while Connor cleaned out some mugs.

She felt suddenly anxious. She'd been meaning to tell him something, tell him when Laurel wasn't there, but now she had the perfect opportunity and she was so uncomfortable it hurt. She breathed in deeply.

"Hey uh Connor, while we're here? Would you be open to me making a personal suggestion for you?"

"You're going to tell me to do the dishes more, aren't you? Laundry!"

"Ha, no, I'm staying the fuck out of those dynamics. It's just with the way... the way you talk and get distracted, and what you told me once about how you could only do well at work if you were doing things your way?"

"Terminally defiant, issues with authority, that's me..."

"I was going to suggest you looked at getting an assessment for ADD. Or just read up about it. It's just a thought really, and you'll get a sense if it's a good fit or not, but I wanted to bring it up in case you hadn't thought about it. It's not all children who can't sit still."

Connor nodded, seeming deep in thought. "I was, indeed, a child who couldn't sit still though! Coffee? Toast?"

Marigold grinned. "I'd actually love both of those if it isn't too much trouble for you."

Marigold appeared at the door to her father's home office.

"One," she said, swinging on one leg, keeping her balance with a hand on the doorframe, "I'm making a cheese toastie for lunch, would you like one? And two, would you be able to give me a ride somewhere tonight?"

Marigold's father looked at her over the propped-up book he had next to his computer. It was a large room for a home office - a second living room, really - but the drafting table and books necessitated it. Midday sunlight streamed in through the window—it was one of the less light rooms in the house but didn't even resemble shaded. Marigold wasn't sure she could ever live at the bottom of a valley like Laurel did. Okay. She would if she had to, but even though her student hostel room and then her studio apartment had been cramped and lacked outside space, there was at least sunlight.

"One, yes please. Two, the last time you asked for a ride you were fourteen. I thought you preferred to do things your own way."

"I do. But I need to negotiate with someone who... has his fingers in a lot of pies, and I think it's important I can get away quickly if I need to."

"Oh Marigold! Marigold Ann Nightfield, what have you got yourself involved in now? No... you can tell me on the way. I'll be your getaway driver... it will make for good stories if nothing else. You know, when you were a teen all my friends thought I had the easy time of it. You didn't drink, you rarely went to parties, you got excellent grades... and you certainly didn't need a getaway driver."

"Oh how the mighty have fallen?" Marigold asked.

"Perhaps. But I was raised by witches, I can be a getaway driver. What time?"

"Leave 9:30?"

"And how far are we going?"

"A warehouse round the back of Johnsonville."

Marigold was surprised to find her hands shaking slightly as she picked fresh basil for the toasties. The evening couldn't come soon enough–and yet she never wanted to have this conversation.

At the address, Marigold flipped the torch on her phone on and walked to the warehouse from the car. Her father wanted to go with her but was reassured by a quick display of magic. It occurred to her that most of this was for show–that there was no actual need to find this guy lurking round a warehouse in the dark, and that thought reassured her a little.

"Clayton Simm?" she asked of the man counting small amounts of cash - really? - at a table just inside the door. He swung round. He was perhaps in his fifties, white and solidly built, with not much hair remaining.

"What if it is?"

Marigold resisted the temptation to roll her eyes.

"I'm told you can arrange to get nanobots created. Under the radar, like."

"I can do many things."

"Good. Because here are the plans. I've done the theoretical work, but I don't have the manufacturing capability."

The man looked down at Marigold. She felt suddenly small, and ridiculous; she still dressed like a child, someone had said, and now she had a feeling this was how she was coming across.

"I assume you know just how expensive this would be?" he said, with a note of deep scepticism. "I assume you have that money. Upfront, ready to put in my bank account."

She had a bit of money. Not enough to get this done legitimately, though, and definitely not enough to deal with whatever the expectation was here. In any case, she wasn't going to show it.

"Do you know what you get in a PhD scholarship living allowance? Less than half the median wage, that's what. If my dad wasn't kindly allowing me to live at home rent-free I don't think I'd have any chance."

"Then why are you wasting my time?"

"Because there are some things rarer than money." Marigold brushed her hands together and orange petals - like her name - appeared from nowhere and then floated slowly off into the distance. "I'm told you have an interest in witchcraft, and I don't exactly see the local witches lining up to help you out."

"There's plenty you don't see. Alright. Are you any good at divining? Dowsing, specifically. There's a property rights issue come up you might be able to help with."

"You want me to find water?"

"I want you to find pipes. Cables. That sort of thing. On a site with a lot of interference. You can do that?"

Marigold shrugged, not wanting it to look to easy or too hard. "Yeah. I can work something out."

"And you'll get your order when it's completed to my satisfaction."

"Sounds like a fair way of doing business. Meanwhile, you feel something warm at the base of your spine?"

"Maybe."

"In the old days, they called that a curse. Think of it like an egg. Not ready to hatch yet. You get me my nanobots, and I'll take it with me. Otherwise, it crawls up your spinal cord. Think of it as more of a snake egg than a chicken one. I'm sure you can work the rest out."

Marigold was still shaking that evening as unloaded the dishwasher, and she wasn't sure whether it was from fear or excitement. She was always the one who was a bit ditzy, coming across younger than she looked, almost naively trusting. She didn't get to drive a hard bargain very often. She didn't get to call people out on their shit and make them agree to her terms. She'd been terrified the whole way through and she didn't want to have to pull shit like this too often but she *liked* the fact she could. And she'd done it successfully.

She wasn't even a strong or experienced witch, and still it had been enough. She hadn't *actually* put a delayed curse on him to be activated if the nanobots weren't delivered, and he didn't really believe she had either. But there was just enough doubt that she was entirely confident the nanobots she had been promised - with the ability to neutralise the existing ones - would be delivered on schedule.

The next morning her alarm woke her up in time for her scheduled video call with Memory. She told her about her fears of losing her magic. Memory had an idea.

"You remember that witchy supplies shop you took me to, once, when we were teenagers, and there was a kid filling in for his grandfather?"

"Not specifically."

"It was where I learned that eye of newt was just mustard seeds. I was terribly disappointed."

"Really. You would prefer actual eyes?"

Memory laughed. "Well not near me, obviously. But the concept seems cool. Anyway, he said he was studying to become a wizard because he didn't have magic innately, but there were ways of learning it. Is that something you could do?"

Marigold laughed. It was so obvious, but she'd never really thought about it. Her family were witches or they were like her, those who could make the odd basic potion. She'd heard of wizards, even met a few, but it didn't seem like something her family did. Suddenly new possibilities and new pathways were opening up in her mind. It wasn't all going to be about loss and endings in the future, just changes. She didn't like change all that much, but she could find ways to grow into it.

But then she thought about losing magic. She wondered if anyone had thought to take proper objective measurements and chart them, and see how different variables influenced them. She opened a new document.

"So," Marigold said. "I actually think it might be you who would benefit from Wizarding classes. You said you were interested in magic, and there are all these magical kids who get really isolated, and you're a teacher."

"Oh no. I cannot open a magical school."

"No. Well, not yet. But what if there were study groups for them? Some sort of online thing? A camp over the summer?"

"Let me have this baby first please," Memory said, but Marigold knew the look on her face. It was the reason they were friends despite not seeming to have that much in common. It was the look of someone making plans.

They started where they had begun, in Otari-Wilton's Bush. It was late morning, overcast, with the wind getting up a bit - it was late summer after all - but for now, at least the rain held off. There were four of them now; Laurel had dragged Connor with her and Marigold invited Neha. It was risky to tell too many people, but she figured she already knew plenty and being secretive just got people's suspicions up.

She had the nanobots in a series of plastic containers. They would need to trial them bit by bit, and try and work out how to distribute them. They started with a patch of plants, and Marigold took a reading showing the strength of these magically powered nanobots. As she already knew, the place was crawling with them.

On Marigold's instruction, Neha knelt down. These bots were bigger than true nanobots; they were just visible with the naked eye, about the size of the poppy seeds the local dairy sold in bulk, claiming they were for baking (the licensing authorities did not buy this reasoning). They were also set to magically vanish after three months, creating no permanent damage to the ecosystem. If this issue wasn't resolved in three months, there were even bigger issues on their hands.

The four of them, crouched on the ground, attracted some occasional looks, but Marigold was quite prepared to say they were students carrying out a field exercise and flash her staff ID card if necessary–and that wasn't even too far from the truth. Neha scattered the bots into the soil as if she were scattering pepper on a meal. Then they waited. Marigold fancied she heard a faint buzzing as the nanobots got to work, but knew that was impossible, that they would not make any sound perceptible to human hearing...

...or was it? She was still a witch. The human brain struggled to interpret all the different new ways of receiving information witches received, and more often than not simplified them into human accessible categories like noise or pain. Either that or they were the closest words for them Marigold had available to her. So it was possible they were working and she was sensing it, but Laurel didn't seem to be reacting to anything. In any case, the true proof would be measured by more precise instruments. Marigold held the scanner over the plants and moved it. She watched the reading reduce.

The others crowded round to watch her—well, Neha and Laurel did, Connor was distracted, trying to talk to a bird.

"It's working," Laurel breathed.

"Seems to be," said Marigold, happily. "We'll test it in a few different areas, and I also want to take some soil samples with nanobots in to be sure it's actually neutralising the problem bots rather than just displacing them, but it's looking promising."

She stood up. It still felt like summer and even with schools back there were plenty of people in the bush, but the winding paths and staggered vegetation meant that it never felt crowded. For a few moments, they had been in their own world, totally absorbed by what they were doing, but now they were back in a public place and at least needed to be somewhat discrete. Marigold distributed small boxes of Nanobots and divided up the areas. They would move out from where they were scattered to cover the whole park, and then go further as necessary.

Marigold walked upwards in the late summer sun, the paths sloping and then turning to steps at one point. She could see over the hills here, even though they weren't high, see the tips of trees branch out amongst the sky. She sat down she off the path, her legs crossed. Before she even opened the nanobots, she tried some magic. She closed her eyes and breathed in, reaching out her hands. Bit by bit small stones edged over to form small conical piles below each hand. She smiled and breathed outwards, and they scattered back to their original positions.

She *was* a witch, and she was connected to what was around her, not just unleashing something foreign upon it. The nanobots would self-destruct eventually. The bush would return to how it was–though, Marigold noted, it was just a small parcel of native bush among hills that were once covered in it. Some wrongs were too great for a witch to undo, but she was doing what she could.

The four of them met back at the entrance to Otari-Wilton's.

"These are for you," Marigold said, holding a small container of her nanobots out to Laurel. "I reckon you're back in business".

All the next day, Marigold was at uni from some ungodly hour in the morning until after midnight, Ubering home in the dark. She didn't hear from Laurel all day, and she didn't message her; she figured she was busy, figured she'd need space. The next day she had a video meeting in the morning with her supervisor who was overseas for three months, and then she took a couple of hours to both write-up notes and recommendations from that while they were still fresh in her mind, and then do some work based on them, ticking off the straightforward things, and starting to explore the more conceptual.

Eventually, her brain had done all it was going to do and Marigold set to work making lemon and thyme marmalade. She zested and boiled the lemons up with sugar, and added thyme just towards the end. On the bench she had a collection of jars, most of them re-used, to pour the marmalade into and let it cool down. It was a good batch, she felt, enough to give a few jars away and have some left to last her the best part of the year. It was a sort of science in itself, stuff like this, something from trial and error and past experience, as well as from measurements and from recipes. Before long she had two large pots of marmalade on the stove - the extractor fan working - and was monitoring the temperature in both with a candy thermometer, waiting for them to reach the next stage.

The thyme came from the garden–still early autumn, and the garden mercifully unaffected. Marigold's fears about it felt like they had been months ago. She didn't know how much longer she'd be staying here, but as long as she was she was determined to keep her grandmother's garden in good shape. It felt like the least she could do really, after everything. Marigold wasn't taking chances though, and she and Laurel had set up some obvious wards on the house. Actually, Marigold didn't know just how many non-obvious wards her grandmother had set up on the house until the time Laurel's Aunt Penelope had visited and immediately spotted them all. Even Laurel herself had missed many, meaning it was a wonder both the monsters and the parasites had been able to get into the house at all.

But Marigold supposed you can't ward effectively against everything. Life would almost be too simple if that were the case.

She set the jars up on the kitchen bench. She'd already printed labels with ingredients and date - not that there were many ingredients but it's always useful for people to know - so she was just about ready.

She opened the door.

"Hey," she said to Laurel, surprised. Laurel normally messaged her before she turned up, firstly because she, y'know, wasn't a boomer and secondly because she knew Marigold needed time to prepare for things. Marigold felt something ache in the pit of her stomach.

As if reading her thoughts, Laurel apologised as she stepped inside.

"I'm sorry, I would have messaged you, I'm just a bit all over the place."

She flopped down on the sofa. She looked exhausted, but at home. Marigold got them both chilled water from the fridge and sat down next to her.

"Are the nanobots working for you?" she asked.

Laurel nodded in response. "I think so. I looked at detector meter and it looks like we got rid of them all. I think the plants are returning to health, but it's not going to be an immediate thing. Hard to tell if I'm just imagining it, but they did look a bit greener this morning. I'll be able to tell in a few days if it's worked for sure but I'm feeling good about it."

"That's good."

"Yeah. Then I'll go back on the cancelled orders once I know if I can fulfil them and offer people a discount if they want to purchase them again, half price I think, keep everyone happy. I'm learning some stuff—especially working with plants, magic or no magic, I'm not in control of everything so I need to do some contingency planning and stuff like that. Not be so taken by surprise."

"You're good at this whole business thing," Marigold said, as Laurel gulped down water. "But to be fair, no-one could exactly blame you for failing to foresee damage caused by a plague of magical nanobots created by a dead witch to try and repair curses on the native ecosystem."

"True. But things always can go wrong and I need to have some sense of how to handle that. But I'll be uh, disguising some of the details in my business plan when I try and get a bank loan to expand next year."

"So you're still serious about it?"

"Hell yeah. I'm treating it as a hobby business and a bit of extra cash just 'til I'm done with uni, but I'm going to have a cooperative witchy plant empire... oh no you're giving that look where you're trying to work out whether to decide to tell me that cooperative and empire are mutually exclusive."

Marigold laughed and blushed. She had totally been thinking exactly that.

"So uh I've been thinking about what you said," Laurel said, in a rush that was more borne from anxiety than a desire to move the conversation along. "I do want to live with you, really I do."

Marigold held her breath and waited for the but.

"And the arguments you made all make sense. My life's been changing a lot lately, though, and I know I wanted things to change, but I also needed to catch my breath. I needed to talk to Connor–he's my best friend, and I didn't want to leave him in the lurch, especially as we once talked about sharing an apartment. I wanted to think everything through. I was also worried about being reliant on you and depending on others. But the more I saw about it the more I realised we're all dependent on others and it's best when we can make good and deliberate choices about how that works."

Marigold nodded. Her brain was whirring ahead, trying to anticipate Laurel's decision, and struggling to hear her words and listen to her properly as her assumptions switched back and forth. She stared at the carpet, fiddling with a rubber band, as she tried to make herself focus.

"So I wanted to suggest how it might work for us and see what you think. Say if I live with you here, I'd need to sort out something for Alfred but I think between our contacts we can work that out. And then while we're here we save. What we'd be paying in rent, or what you can afford if it's not in your budget. Come the end of the year I'll be done with my Masters and have more time to work on the business, and you'll have handed your thesis in for marking."

Marigold tried very hard to not display obvious panic at that statement, and instead let Laurel continue.

"Which means, end of the year, we'll be in a good position to rent an apartment together. Something not mouldy even."

"The pinnacle of the Wellington rental market!" Marigold said, raising her glass of water. "And I can still come back to take care of the garden - I guess long term Dad's probably going to end up selling this place anyway, so I need to work that out. But yeah. Y'know, everything you're saying sounds good. Amazing even. Oh my god, this is going to be so fun, we can get some new art prints for the walls. Oh and Sorrel will be coming to stay with *both* of us now, we'll have a spare room all set up for them."

And Laurel, finally, was calm and smiling, and Marigold curled up against her. They'd done good.

Marigold stayed over at Laurel's that night. She knew that Laurel was going to miss this place but it surprised her to realise she would as well. Not in a way that cancelled out, y'know, liveable standard of housing, but she would. She thought about this awake early again, lying in the dark, feeling Laurel's body next to hers, listening to the sound of the wind around them, and of the monster under the floor.

In the morning, they had breakfast with Connor and Leilani. When she walked into the kitchen Connor was juggling the fruit from the fruit bowl. Laurel came through with her laptop.

"So, ballet tickets. Does the fifteenth sound okay to you?"

But Marigold had other things occupying her mind as well. Even though the succulents issue was largely resolved, it had set off her mind in a bunch of new directions–as if she needed any more, and she was only just starting to run through them properly now. She was thinking about all the ways magic could be used to *benefit* the ecosystem. She probably needed to talk to Laurel's brother about that - he was probably way ahead of her on the subject - but she'd like to hear what was going on, and she might even have the odd useful idea, potentially.

She was thinking about all this on her way home, and her thoughts were only interrupted by the box on her doorstep–an unexpected package. Toad leapt out of her pocket excitedly to sit on it.

There was a note on top of the box. Marigold edged Toad over so she could read it.

This may seem odd because I know you've just been working on destroying Thomas's work. But we think you'd have got on–you both care about science and magic and the world we live in. We'll invite you and Laurel for dinner when we're not spending all our time on housing renovations, but in the meantime, we think Thomas would want you to have this. Tay, Aishah and Adam.

Marigold tore open the box, and among the packaging she found a microscope and gasped. The microscope was, at a guess, early nineteenth century, a dark red with brass fixings, beautifully polished. She'd never seen one that looked so perfect. Marigold held it carefully in her hands. It didn't have a fraction of the magnification power of the one in her lab, let alone those she had access to at uni. But it had other power. Power of history. Power of having successfully made new connections. And maybe...

She turned it over in her hands and felt it almost vibrate within them. Yes, a different power. Definitely a bit of magic.

Magic on the Waves

This bonus festive short story is set between the events of Succulents and Spells and Microscopes and Magic.

"In the freezer. Not on top, *in* the freezer. It's not going to stay cold up there."

The familiar voice floated out of the house. Laurel brought the car to a stop and paused for a moment parked up beside the open door, her hands on the steering wheel, grinning at the comforting familiarity of her Auntie Marcia trying to create some order amid the chaos. Cousins were milling around the back garden of the old house, not far from Papamoa's beach; snacks were on tables, tents already pitched.

"You ready?" she said to Marigold, who was looking slightly dazed. It had been a long journey up; the roads were typically busy just a few days out from Christmas.

Marigold nodded, not saying anything. Laurel hoped she wasn't too overwhelmed. The first Christmas with your partner's family was a big deal in anyone's book. And Marigold wasn't exactly used to families like this.

The moment Laurel opened the door her cousin Jarred came hurtling towards her, trapping her in a bear hug. Two years younger than her, they'd grown up together, more siblings than cousins. It had been too long since she last saw him. And then Auntie Marcia was there too, her wavy blonde hair cut to a bob, looking happy but a little stressed. Laurel didn't blame her.

Auntie Marcia was technically her first cousin, but pre-ciseness didn't count for much; everyone was family. She'd only moved into this house – Gran's house – a couple of years back, after her divorce. It meant Gran had people looking out for her and help taking care of the big old house, and Marcia and her three kids weren't wasting most of their money on ever-growing rental prices for increas-ingly poor quality houses. This place was old, but it was dry and clean, and didn't involve pouring money into someone else's pocket.

"You're *sure* you don't mind sleeping outside," Marcia asked Laurel and Marigold, a touch of concern in her voice.

"Wouldn't be Christmas if we weren't in some tent as the wind howled around us," Laurel said. "Seriously, I'm only 27, not old and decrepit yet."

"Oy, watch what you're implying!"

"We've got plenty of gear," Marigold interjected, a smile on her face, playing the peacemaker.

"Ok. Well, it's lovely to meet you Marigold, and to see you again Laurel. You should come up more often. Your parents are getting a motel, did they tell you – they'll be here tomorrow. I've put the boys in together so my mum can take their room, Ash and Frieda are with their baby in the spare room, Arry and Rose have the attic, Lyndon is on the sofa because he hates camping and has promised me he'll be up and put his stuff away by eight each morning and I'm the sort of idiot who believes that. Gran's in her usual room, of course, and the rest of you are camping or just visiting for the day. Oh, except I've let Sorrel keep... their room because they're having a bit of a time. Your parents updated you on Sorrel?"

"Sorrel, they/them pronouns, got it!" Laurel said, giving a thumbs up. She turned to Marigold. "Marcia's twelve-year-old, my cousin. New name, new pronouns – some of the family are adjusting a bit."

Marigold smiled.

"Looking forward to meeting them."

Laurel turned back to Marcia who was absent-mindedly moving her bracelet round in circles on their wrist.

"Don't worry, this isn't new to us. Are they doing okay?"

Marcia shrugged, lowering her voice. "I don't know. I looked up some stuff online and all it said was if you love and accept your kid they'll be fine but... they're not happy. Quite withdrawn. And we *do* love and accept them. I had to get used to changing how I spoke about them but I'm much better at it now. It hasn't helped."

"It's not just you though," Laurel said, waving their hand, indicating the town, the long beach, the whole world. "It's everything. I'll have a talk to them."

"Oh would you, please?"

"Of course."

Marigold opened the back of the car, looking around then speaking conspiratorially to Laurel as they started to unpack.

"She knows we're cis right? I mean you, obviously, but does she read me as trans...?" Marigold grinned, running her hand over her freshly buzzcut hair.

"Nah. We're gay and we're from Wellington, so I think in their eyes it comes to the same thing. And hey, we've been through coming out and all that. It's not the same, but we can be of help. And we have enough non-binary friends that they won't need to explain themselves. Either way, they're my baby cousin and I want them to know we have their back.

Marigold made affirmative noises as she dragged the tent out of the boot, followed by what was definitely excessive equipment for a week of backyard camping. Fortunately, there was plenty of lawn – this house was an old homestead, built long before most of the town, and the family had resisted plenty of subdivision offers from developers.

In the evening, Jarred picked up fish and chips for the whole family and they ate together, crowded on a mosaic of blankets. Laurel leaned back in the afternoon sun, happy; this was her family, and now Marigold was here everything felt complete. For her part, Marigold had found the scientists in the family and was babbling happily about developments in the speed of genetic sequencing, listening to a spiel about the possibility of solar-powered commercial flights in return. Laurel shouldn't have been worried. This was a family of people who always felt they had to be a little outside regular society, and a family where weird and specialised interests were the norm. Even aside from her temporary magical ability Marigold fit right in.

They swam that night. Marigold needed some decompression time, lying in the tent with her sunglasses and noise cancelling headphones on. Laurel agreed it was a good idea to digest the meal properly first. So, in the still-light evening, Laurel leant against the outside of the house, trailed her fingers around the wood, felt the magic of generations reverberating in it. She knew a witch could live anywhere, but magic built up over time in places like this. She wondered if soon it would be time to travel, time for her to follow her ancestry.

Marigold appeared then, and in seconds they'd got themselves into their togs in the dim light of their tent, wrapped towels around themselves, and were heading barefoot down to the beach, over the sand dunes and into the sea. The water was warm in the cold air and they ran in easily, the world smelling of salt and summer.

Laurel took a few strokes out, long and strong, reaching out into the bay and then turned until she was parallel to the sand. She knew this beach well, knew its traps and shifts of sand. Marigold wasn't far behind her, in bright purple and white patterned togs, a contrast to Laurel's sleek black swimsuit.

The summer and the years stretched out for Laurel. She was at the start of something good, she knew it. She'd quit her exhausting job, she had Marigold, Connor – her sort of flatmate but sort of brother – who was doing a lot better at his business and correspondingly being less annoying. She was going to finally tick off the box of finishing her MA – not because she was planning to do anything with it, but because it hung over her like a dark, unfinished cloud, a sink of time and money with nothing to show for it.

Most importantly, her nascent business was going well – she'd been selling her succulents and the fairs, and word of mouth had got out. She'd joined forces with a pottery witch whose pots perfectly encouraged the growth of the succulents, perfectly adapting in shape and size, and colour to show them off best. Her magic worked so gradually that no-one would notice that there was any magic happening at all... they'd just know that they felt very good about the purchase and without being able to put in words what was so good about it, they'd start recommending them to all their friends.

Laurel charged a lot for the succulents, and for some reason that attracted people rather than putting them off, making them believe that maybe she was selling something truly special. They understood special even if they didn't understand magical... at least not magical in its literal meaning, anyway.

Laurel let herself float in the sea for a while, moving just enough to keep herself afloat, allowing herself to move with the waves. The afternoon sun was dying into twilight and the town was lighting up, all the way along the long beach and over towards the Mount at one side, and out to open land and water at the other. There were few out this late, but come New Year the water would be busy, even in the evenings. But now it was quiet enough that they could pretend the beach was theirs.

The peace was interrupted by splashes behind them. Laurel turned, just in time to get a glimpse of a child swimming strongly along the water. It was hard to get a good view of them because they splashed up water as they went, making their curls look blue in some trick of the light. They swam with confidence, not even seeming to notice Laurel or Marigold, as if perfectly comfortable with the world around them.

Laurel turned her head back to look at Marigold. She had an odd feeling, something she couldn't quite put her finger on, the sense that maybe magic was involved.

"Bit late for a kid to be out alone?" she said, uncertainly.

"They seem a strong swimmer." Marigold sounded more confident than Laurel felt. She knew Marigold had spent a lot of time alone as a kid, and seemed okay about that but something didn't quite sit well with Laurel. The two of them swam in the direction the kid had been, but there was nothing. No sign of distress, nor a child heading to shore.

"Yeah," Laurel said eventually. "I'd have sensed if someone was in trouble – if I didn't know that I'd have called in a report. I've had to do that before, wasn't fun. So it must be fine it just... feels weird."

They grabbed their towels and headed back over the dunes. A few metres away, in the middle of the sharp hardy grass, was Sorrel, overdressed for the weather in a hoodie and jeans, kicking the sand.

"Hey Sorrel," Laurel called.

Sorrel turned and looked directly at them, but it was almost as though they didn't register either of them were there. After a few seconds Sorrel turned back to determinedly kicking at the sand.

"They're not usually like this," said Laurel, and Marigold only nodded.

Back at the house, their muscles pleasantly aching and towels wrapped around them, Laurel and Marigold shrugged off the last of the sun.

Tibbs yowled as they came through the gate.

"I've already fed all the cats," Marnie yelled.

Laurel shook her head disapprovingly at her familiar, then reached down to scratch his chin. "We're onto your lies, my friend."

They slept early and deeply that night, tired from the drive. The wind was gentle around the tent – a nice contrast to Wellington's howling gales where Laurel would not have even considered pitching a tent; either it would fly away or they'd die in the night when a rogue trampoline blew into them. Up here, in Papamoa, it felt like people didn't have to worry about anything, certainly not flying trampolines.

Laurel laughed to herself, quietly; Marigold was already asleep, a leg and an arm sprawled across Laurel's space, the sound of her breathing almost in time with the wind. They'd been together less than six months but she felt like part of the family. Laurel found she was holding her breath, not daring to hope. She saw more Christmases like this, stretching out into the future. She saw her bringing Marigold into this ridiculous growing family, of holidays spent flung together in attics or camping on lawns. Of wandering, just the two of them, round by the beach, up hills to watch the stars.

Laurel fell asleep like that, but when she dreamed it was not of romantic futures together, but of chasing a child desperately through the water, a child she didn't know and yet was somehow desperately important to her, and every time she got close a wave crashed down and tore the child from her grasp.

The following day was equally chaotic – in fact, Laurel expected little but chaos the whole time they were there. Everyone seemed to be up to something, even Gran – resulting in Marcia threatening more than once to send her off to Ravensdown. But somehow there was always plenty of food – there were trips out for takeaways or bread or ice blocks or to refill the gas canisters for the barbeque, and if it was punctuated by yelling and hammering on bathroom doors, well, that was just how Christmas was.

They read for a while on the beach and then swam in the afternoon that day. There was no sign of the child they'd seen in the water; and no reports of anyone missing either; Laurel had checked with a lifeguard. It seemed it was all nothing; a child, perhaps older than they'd appeared, who was perhaps taking a risk out for a night swim. Perhaps they sneaked out without their parents knowing. Laurel felt sure someone would have raised the alarm by now if a child had not returned home, but something... something felt wrong.

Once they were back, in the middle of the chaos, Laurel suddenly felt the need to be in fresh clothes.

"Hey Sorrel do you mind if we borrow your room to get changed in."

"As long as you don't leave it a mess."

"Sorrel's room," Marcia said, conspiratorially, "is always immaculate. We never have any arguments about tidying it. They're a paragon of cleanliness."

Sorrel rolled their eyes. Their hair – mousy brown – was curly and not much longer than a bob but in consideration of the summer heat had been somehow forced it into a short ponytail. They were lounging in orange leggings and a white t-shirt with a cartoon character Laurel didn't recognise on.

"We'll be careful. Promise."

Sorrel's room was at once what might be called *shambolic*, and tidier than Laurel would have expected. If she had to choose one word it would have been bright, because there was an influx of colours from every direction, clusters around the room; one of nail polish, one of the construction toys they'd not yet outgrown, one of socks. Everything was on display, or more accurately heaped in piles; there was not a closed drawer in sight.

But Sorrel was clearly, as Laurel had long suspected, a witch, and their interests as displayed in this room confirmed that: crystals on an altar, a few beginners' books, the scent of herbs and a few packets of them in cloth around the place. It reminded Laurel of her own teens, her scattered attempts at learning witchcraft under the guidance of family members whose tutoring was well-meant but erratic, and sometimes very contradictory.

But she wasn't here to snoop. Laurel dried and threw on a comfortable summer dress quickly, well aware they were taking advantage of the goodwill of a preteen – and in her experience preteens sometimes had limited goodwill to offer. In about the same amount of time, Marigold was in denim shorts and a t-shirt with a maths joke on it that Laurel didn't understand even after the first time Marigold had tried to explain it to her.

Dressed and their towels hung up with countless others on the line to dry, Laurel read a book in the garden while Marigold was demonstrating her magic progress to – and receiving some tips from – Gran. With only months' worth of magical ability, Marigold had made solid progress, but unease hung over her sometimes. Her magic powers would not last forever – she was not a true witch and in months or maybe a few years they would fade to nothing. She'd said she wasn't sure whether to carry on as if they weren't there, or to make the most of them in the little time she had.

And Marigold had plenty to do, with her PhD and her off-the-record magical scientific experiments, without adding learning magic into the mix, especially if it could disappear any moment and have all been for nothing.

Laurel hoped Marigold was okay with spending the whole Christmas and New Year with Laurel's family and away from her own. She'd certainly *said* she was fine in it, but there had been a bit of a distant look in her eyes as she'd said that. In any case, in the New Year they were going to stop by and visit Marigold's mother in Napier for a couple of days, before heading back down to Wellington. Things were changing. Laurel had already enrolled in her MA, and she was going to finish it this time, hell or high water. Laurel only hoped Marigold was going to stay a part of that change.

At night, while the children were asleep, some of them gathered round a fire pit. Lyndon lit the wood with a flick of his fingers, and it sparked into life, flames licking upwards and sparks exploding in the night. Laurel rolled her eyes.

"Show off," she said, knowing that it took more energy to light with magic than the normal way, but everyone ignored her, sitting back and feeling the heat of the fire, watching the orange spit into the dark air. It was a comfortable warmth; Marigold and Laurel shared a blanket over their knees, but felt quite okay with bare arms. It was a clear night, and the stars here were brighter than in Wellington. A few beers were passed around but no-one talked much. After the busy day, it was time to just hang out.

The whole family took muffins and coffee down to the beach the next morning. Laurel was no fan of cold morning swims and stayed on the beach, but Marigold went for a quick dip and returned with her eyes shining, shaking droplets of water from her not-very-much hair that sparkled in the sun. The kids headed to the water quickly, of course, but the rest of them lounged on the beach. Laurel had a novel and Marigold a game on her phone that she was idly colour matching shapes on, chroma orders of colours that were very closely matched.

About a third of the people present were witches, and that meant familiars – as well as the regular pets that lived here. Tibbs was just old and grumpy and spent his time lurking in the sharp grass of the sand dunes, eyeing up birds he knew better than to catch. Some had gone off exploring, others – like Marigold's frog – stayed with her most of the time, though it did seem to have a rather deep aversion to saltwater, and burrowed in the sand when Marigold went swimming. Soap, on the other hand, appeared not to bother it one bit, which had caused some issues when Marigold had helped do the dishes or, worse, when someone else had been doing them.

Marcia was making some of the men do lunch prep and clean up for once and told Laurel she wasn't needed. Marigold had gone off to buy coffee and a few other things. It was a good time for Laurel to talk to her cousin.

Sitting on their bed, Sorrel picked up their own familiar – a tunnel-web spider – up and let it crawl across their face. Their nails had pink glitter polish and it sparkled as it caught the sun.

"I like your new name," Laurel said, feeling a flush of awkward on her face. "It's a good witch name."

"It is. I wouldn't have given myself a bad witch name." Sorrel was the opposite of the withdrawn kid Laurel had been led to expect; they were brimming with a wild confidence and a wicked sarcasm that Laurel couldn't remember having at that age, or ever to be honest.

"And the rest of the family are getting it right and stuff? And your pronouns?"

"They're doing okay. Even gran gets my name right most of the time, though pronouns are a bit hard for her. I wish there were more kids like me at school but we've got an online group and there's a youth group in Tauranga Mum's going to drive me to in the New Year sometimes."

"So you're feeling okay?"

"Yeah. The only problem is that Mum won't let me get a spray bottle like you have for cats to squirt people who misgender me."

Laurel stifled a giggle. "I have to say I can see both sides here."

"Of course you can. That's what old people do."

"Hey! Is this trip just going to be people calling me old? I'm twenty-seven!"

"That's pretty old... did they have the internet when you were a kid?"

"Thanks Sorrel! You're my favourite."

"Welcome."

"So uh your mum said you'd seemed a bit unhappy. Hiding in your room, that sort of thing. That's not because of your identity?"

"Agender people are allowed out, you know."

"Yes, I know that. Just. Okay, when I was young, when dinosaurs roamed the earth as you'd put it, I worked out I was queer really young but I was really scared of people finding out. I didn't tell anyone except my best friend until I moved to Wellington – and I couldn't tell you exactly why. Yes, I knew I'd get shit at school, but I also knew my parents would be supportive, which is better than a lot of people have it – and it was worse then, believe me. But I just... struggled with it. I think I'd absorbed a lot of bad things about myself without realising it. I felt terrible. Does any of that sound familiar?"

Sorrel shook their head slowly.

"I guess it was hard when I didn't have a name for what was going on for me, and I was scared of telling people at first, but now people know... No, it's fine. I feel good about it. It feels good to be me."

"And you've got friends who support you?"

Sorrel shrugged. "There are a lot of old people here. Like really old not just like you. But the kids at school are ok. We hang out."

Laurel suddenly had another thought. "Any strong swimmers? We saw a kid about your age in the water swimming way out, on their own. They seemed to almost disappear into the water, but I could tell they weren't in trouble. It was weird."

Laurel caught something distant and scared in Sorrel's eye, but only for a second.

"We all swim a bit because we live by the beach," Sorrel said hurriedly. "I don't know anyone super into swimming..."

Laurel wanted to ask more but already they were being called down for lunch. "It's good you're doing okay," she said, squirting hand sanitiser on her hands and passing the bottle to Sorrel. "You let me know if you need me, okay."

They swam again in the evening, hitting the warm sea from the cooling air. Most of them were at the beach – most of the younger adults, anyway, and the sun had not yet hit the horizon. Some of them sat on the beach with beer that wasn't nearly as well hidden as they thought it was, but most got at least a bit of a swim in.

Laurel and Marigold took it slowly, more wading and messing around than actual swimming, allowing themselves to float and move in the buoyancy of the warm sea that surrounded them. But then Marigold pointed out to sea and Laurel followed the line of her finger until she saw exactly what Laurel was pointing at.

The same child swimming far out to sea, on the horizon.

Laurel had had enough. She was going to solve this one.

"Watch me," she said to Marigold, knowing she was going further out than she'd been in a long time. She was a good swimmer, had grown up with summers at the beach and still made it to the Freyberg or Thorndon pools most weeks, but she knew the water could be dangerous, knew rips could form or muscles cramp. She could have gone back and done some spells, made potions for strength or something, but she was worried the child would be gone by then, so she ran into the water until it reached her armpits, and then she swam.

Her arms moved fast, one after the other, pushing her forward over the waves. She left behind the cluster of late swimmers, left behind the beach, and she was out into the sea, blinking away saltwater, pushing against the tide. She could still keep sight of the child swimming, and she felt she was getting a little closer, but everything was further away and longer to reach than she had anticipated.

And then, almost without thinking, Laurel was face to face with what she had been chasing all along.

She tried to say something, but her words kept leaving her as she tried to process exactly what it was she was seeing in front of her. She trod water, let herself float a bit while trying to take in the head and shoulders that emerged from the waves in front of her.

The child was not human, that was for sure. They glistened like water had been given a cohesive form, like ice that had just melted and yet kept its shape. Blue-shite, semi-translucent, their curls tumbled down around their face, their eyes focused on swimming.

They were not like anything Laurel had seen before, but their features, their expression, that messy hair, that was all unmistakeably familiar.

"Sorrel?" Laurel said, realising as she did so that she was almost out of breath. She reached out to take the water child by the shoulder, and her hand fell through the water with no resistance. The child was swimming away, disappearing into the horizon faster than Laurel could ever swim, and was gone.

Back on dry land, catching her breath, wrapping her towel around her, Laurel tried to process what she'd seen, tried to explain to Marigold. It was hard to put in context, to square up with other things she'd seen or done. The closest thing she was able to relate it to was making a mirror. Making a mirror was showy, impressive to those not in the know – certainly not as vague and simple as a herbal poultice, for example. But it was something many witches were taught early, and one of Laurel's grandmother's (and Sorrel's great grandmother's) favourite tricks. A mirror was really just a hallucination, something that looked illusionarily like the person who had created it, but was not alive in any real way. It could mimic a few movements or retell that which the person had in the past, and would not last long – a few hours perhaps. Good for showing off, good for pranks, probably completely useless for anything other than that.

But, intentional or not, something had happened very differently here. And it was beginning to make sense why Sorrel hadn't exactly been all sunshine and laughter lately.

"Looks like we've got a summer mystery to solve," Laurel said to Marigold, slipping her feet into her jandals before climbing over the dunes with their sharp grass, Marigold following her.

"Don't talk about it with anyone," Laurel cautioned Marigold. "We'll bring people in if we need to but if Sorrel has fucked something up and already feels bad about it I sure as hell don't want to make that any worse."

"Got it," said Marigold, as they turned the corner and took the shortcut back to the big house with the long garden behind it, the fruit trees and the beehives right down at the far end by the stream. Laurel was aching a little after the swim, but it was the good ache of summer exertion and she was, despite the knowledge they were about to face something that would be at the very least awkward, and possibly dangerous, happy. Summer did that to you; the smell of salt and sun in everything, and now she had someone else to share it with.

And it wouldn't be a family Christmas without some episode of magic gone wrong. One of Laurel's first memories was the "use magic to speed up the cooking of meringue" incident, which ended up in the whole kitchen filled with crisp, ever-expanding egg whites. Then there was the year that ended with half of Papamoa calling in the floating fireball as a UFO, and the time every toy vehicle in the house began moving independently – and not according to any traffic management system.

In short, Sorrel was basically going through a rite of passage. The only thing that was really concerning Laurel was how different it was from anything she had seen before... and the uncanny sense that the person she had seen in the water was more than just an illusion to them. There was a depth to them that she had never seen before in a mirror. A sense of personality.

She was going to have to talk to Sorrel.

It was Christmas Eve and Sorrel was making noises about being too old for a stocking while at the same time firmly hanging it up by the fireplace when Laurel finally got the chance to talk to them alone.

"I need to get a few things from the supermarket. Can you come and give me a hand?"

Sorrel shrugged. "Okay," they said, unenthused. Not that Laurel blamed them. Laurel made up a shopping list in her head as Sorrel strapped themself into the car – Marigold's father's car really, and Laurel was not looking forward to not having use of the very good quality vehicle when he returned in the new year.

"So," Laurel said, once they were driving. "You cast a mirror spell? Well done."

Sorrel shrugged and looked away, perhaps gauging how much Laurel had worked out, how much they could get away with not saying.

"Mirror spells are awesome," Laurel continued. "It's really frustrating when you're first learning witchcraft. You spend hours trying to light a fire with your fingers until you cry, and then you have Gran standing over you checking you measure rosemary exactly right and trying to remember which spells you stir clockwise and which anti-clockwise, but then suddenly everything comes together and you can really make things happen. And making a mirror is the coolest of those. Sure, it's an illusion really, but it makes you feel like you're a real witch."

Sorrel wasn't crying, not quite. Laurel softened her voice.

"What did you do differently, Sorrel? Why is your mirror made of water? Why won't they go away?"

Sorrel choked. "I didn't want to say because it sounds so stupid."

"Hey. I'll tell you some stories of my own stupidity one day. If your brothers don't already tell them at the dinner table."

Sorrel's lip twitched with slight amusement, despite themself.

"Sea salt," they said. "Instead of regular. It seemed fancier than the stuff Mum uses on the slugs, and it's just the same chemical formula, right, so it should be the same. But it wasn't..."

"Ah," Laurel said. "You need to talk to Marigold. She has that whole scientific approach to magic, but most of the time it doesn't work like that. Did you do anything else differently?"

Sorrel shook their head and Laurel, finding a park in a busy supermarket car park, contemplated quietly. The sea salt would account for the different form of the illusion. But not for its persistence. A mirror lingers, close to you, for a few hours, maybe enough time for you to yell for your family and show them excitedly. It does not go off on its own for days or more.

But there was no need to scare Sorrel, not just yet.

"Come on," she said, and Sorrel unbuckled themself and took the trolley while Laurel grabbed chippies and sausages and another pack of napkins.

Christmas day dawned in the Windflower house with the usual measure of chaos and excitement. There were few children at the moment – a baby and nine-year-old twins were the only ones younger than Sorrel – and Laurel and Marigold ignored the jibes about a new generation arriving before too long.

Laurel knew the older witches in the family would have spent weeks working spells in preparation; spells for harmony and goodwill, spells for everyone getting enough sleep to not grouch at the family in the morning, spells for nothing getting burned and remembering to refill the gas bottles on time. What magic was worked on Christmas day, though, was pure showing off. Lights sparkled in the air to form pictures, ice cream containers were opened to find the ice cream neatly arranged in scoops, raspberries floated through the air to arrange themselves on pavlova.

Marigold, after volunteering twice to help, was put on shelling peas duty outside with Sorrel, the two of them sitting cross-legged over a large saucepan, the peapods on a sheet of newspaper to one side. Laurel was inside, putting together a pear, walnut and goats cheese salad, and then spooning sorbet into glasses. There was no formal meal, just an endless circuit of food and drinks and laughs. The weather was on their side.

Of course it was – they were witches!

Laurel was not as relaxed as she normally was. She and Marigold had been up late working on the spell, and at last she thought she had something that would work. It was hard enough even to get Sorrel alone in the middle of the chaos – Sorrel had to explain the plans as she picked basil leaves to go with the tomato and mozzarella skewers, mint for the ginger wine.

Somehow, though, the three of them managed to put together what they needed and leg it across the road and the dunes. They left their towels and their jandals on the sand, and ran into the sea. The sun was high in the sky and if they didn't know what they needed to do, it would have felt just like one more day of the holiday.

At first, there was no sign of the child in the water, and Laurel began to worry if this was all for nothing. They swam further out though, and there they were, long limbs and curly hair. This time they did not turn away but turned to face them.

It was remarkable, up close, how good a mirror this was. In any other circumstances, it would have been a sign of magical talent. But there was no time for that now. They had to solve this; for now the only negative effect was the worry it was causing Sorrel, but it was only a matter of time before this kid triggered a full-scale search operation.

Laurel had the eucalyptus oil and the sage and the black pepper in a little packet secured to her wrist with a rubber band and she emptied the contents over the person in the water, but that was all she could do.

All that was left was for Sorrel to push through their emotional block, the fears that had been holding them back.

"You can do it," Laurel whispered.

Sorrel held out their hands, but nothing happened. Laurel and Marigold tried to be patient, moving with every wave.

"Just a bit more," Marigold said.

"I'm *trying*." Sorrel sounded near tears, as frustrated as the rest of them. They yelled something indistinguishable, and then the wave came, crashing down on them, and Laurel reached for Marigold, reached for her cousin as she plunged downwards into the water.

Holding her breath and pulling herself upwards, she found the surface again, choking, Marigold seemingly unphased, holding up Sorrel.

"You okay?" Marigold asked. but Laurel was looking behind her, at the massive spiral of water circling into the air like a tornado, heading for the clouds.

Laurel swore and recited the first spell she could think of which mercifully drew it down towards them before it disappeared into the ocean.

"What was that," Marigold asked.

"Not what our spell was meant to do. Let's get to shore, now."

A small crowd was looking in their direction as they came close to shore but they dispersed as soon as Jarred and a couple of other family members came running across the beach. Laurel could recognise a distraction spell when she saw one.

"I'm sorry..." Sorrel started to say.

"Hey, no need to apologise. You... oh no!"

"What?" Marigold asked, to Laurel who was looking at the figure walking slowly across the dunes.

"It's Gran. I'm for it now."

Gran didn't walk as fast as she used to, especially on the sand, and it felt like each step she made drew out the fear for Laurel. She'd truly messed this one up. She had been just beginning to think she was no longer the disappointing witch in the family.

"Who is going to explain to me," Gran said. "Just what happened here."

Laurel stepped forward, giving a brief recounting while Sorrel stared at their feet.

"So I don't know if it's because they're... experiencing a fractured sense of self, or they feel torn between identities, or if it's a desire to be somewhere else entirely..."

Gran rolled her eyes.

"I wish you'd told me about this earlier. You're as bad as Marcia, always fretting about psychology this and psychology that. There's nothing wrong with this one – nothing more than a bit of smart talk, and weren't we all as bad at that age?"

"Then what..."

Gran looked at Sorrel.

"I was going to let you get away with it, but it seems the situation has changed. That memory spell you tried to help with your exams... no don't bother denying it, we've all done it. Did you clean your tools properly afterwards?"

Sorrel looked desperate for a sinkhole to open beneath them.

"I can't hear you."

"Maybe... maybe not as well as I should have done."

Gran looked victorious.

"See! You can tell them once, you can tell them a thousand times, but the only way a child will listen is when something like this happens. Ok, so eucalyptus was a good thought but this is really about memory at the centre of it..."

Jarred was sent back to the house to get herbs, Sorrel was taught what to recite and how to focus. Laurel and Marigold wrapped themselves in towels and sat on the beach. Most of the family had joined them by this time – which probably didn't help Sorrel's confidence any but they knew better than to complain.

At last, Sorrel walked alone into the sea. Laurel calmed the waves around them, just a little. Marigold saw it first, the water person, the mirror, walking through the sea towards them.

"You can do it," Laurel whispered, even though their cousin could not hear her.

Sorrel was neck deep, still standing, reached out to the water form of themself that mirrored her entirely, grasped her hands. They said words in earnest that Laurel couldn't make out over the sound of the waves, and then for a moment there were the two of them facing each other.

The family exchanged glances, unsure what was meant to happen, and then the mirror-self started swimming away from Sorrel. Gran took two firm steps towards the water, evidently concerned.

But then Sorrel was swimming too, arms flying one after another, catching up on this version of themself, grabbing them, holding them, yelling something indistinguishable and then...

...and then the mirror became simply water, slipping through Sorrel's arms. Laurel picked up a towel and draped it over her cousin's shoulders as they walked back to shore.

"Happy Christmas," Marigold said, laughing, and Sorrel rolled their eyes but walked back with them across the sand, which was the clearest indicator they were once again a regular pre-teen.

Their time in Papamoa over, Laurel and Marigold drove down to Hawke's Bay. Marigold had given Laurel an undercut with her clippers and her hair felt light in the summer breeze through the car window.

"So what were you talking to Marcia about?" Laurel asked, speeding up on the open road.

"Sorrel's going to come visit for a few days. Even when Dad's back we've got plenty of space."

"Are you kidding?" Laurel asked. "She's never let any of the kids stay with me – thinks I'm up to all sorts."

Marigold laughed. "Well, she's clearly decided I'm somehow trustworthy. I promised to show them around the biology department and help build, and I quote, aspiration for their future studies. A week of showing Sorrel round the city? I reckon we can do that."

"We're going to end up eating so much ice cream if we're charged with an almost-thirteen-year-old, y'know."

"Already thought of that. So we'll start with the place on Cuba Street, and then the gelato on the waterfront and then..."

Marigold's voice faded into the quiet hum of the electric engine. Maybe some of the family had them designated as old, but neither of them were quite ready to concede to that. Not just yet.

"Remember the Ben and Jerry's pop-up they had at civic square one year," Marigold said, her voice suddenly loud again. Laurel didn't need to reply, just leaned back into the passenger seat and felt the breeze ripple over her hair.

A note from Andi R. Christopher

Thanks so much for reading! I really enjoyed writing this sequel to *Succulents and Spells*, along with the Christmas short story "Magic on the Waves" which was originally published in the *Jingle Spells* anthology along with work by some other Witchy Fiction authors. Do head to https://witchyfiction.com to see what all the other authors are up to.

I've brought this series to sit under my new pen name, Andi R. Christopher. Same me, just trying to keep similar books together so it's easier for you to find more of what you love. Huge thanks to Anna, Toni, Helen, Jamie and everyone else for your help and support.

The series is now complete, following Laurel and Marigold, and two other witchy couples, over five books. If you want to meet a new couple, with a bonus appearance from Laurel and Marigold, check out Alpaca and Apparitions.

I've also started a new series set in Aotearoa New Zealand. It's filled with sea magic and mystery, following a young woman as she discovers her powers. It starts with Tides of Magic, available from all the usual retailers.

Lastly, I'd love to keep in touch with you via my newsletter. You can subscribe at https://andi.digitalpress.blog/ . And if you liked *Succulents and Spells*, please consider reviewing it on Goodreads or your ebook site of choice. Every review helps!

About the author

Andi R. Christopher is a writer of queer urban and contemporary fantasy. Their Charley Deacon series – stories of sea magic and self discovery – begins with "Tides of Magic", out now, and their previous Windflower series comprises cosy novellas about queer witches in Aotearoa New Zealand. They also write speculative fiction as Andi C. Buchanan. You can find them online at andirchristoph er.com or https://linktr.ee/andiwrites.

Also by Andi R. Christopher

Windflower Series

Succulents and Spells

Microscopes and Magic

Alpaca and Apparitions

Data and Divination

Weddings and Witchcraft

Charley Deacon Series

Tides of Magic

Tides of Change